No love was lost between nifer Grey. After he was fired from the o sabotage her career. They hadn't spoken i t when he turns up dead after sending a cryptic m o his supposed enemy, Jennifer senses foul play. Add the death of Bobby's girl friend and the strange appearance of a dozen of his reporter's note-books, and the case turns decidedly bizarre. Deciphering Bobby's notes turns out to be the deciding factor.

Jerry B. Jenkins, is the author of more than fifty books, including the popular Margo Mystery Series, co-author of the best-selling *OUT OF THE BLUE* with Orel Hershiser, and *HEDGES*. Jenkins lives with his wife Dianna, and three sons at Three-Son Acres, Zion, Illinois.

# Jerry B. Jenkins

# TOO LATE TO TELL

### Book Three In The Jennifer Grey Mystery Series

Flip over for another great
Jennifer Grey Mystery!
**GATEWAY**

**BARBOUR BOOKS**
Westwood, New Jersey

# TOO LATE TO TELL

# One

As much as Jennifer Grey disliked Bobby Block, his mysterious note intrigued her.

He had always been a young man of complex problems, one she had never been able to figure. Clearly, he had always envied her, and after only a brief period of conniving, he showed his true colors and tried openly to destroy her. But Jennifer had survived.

Bobby had been a hulking, earnest, dark-haired graduate student from Northwestern University's Medill School of Journalism when they had met. He was already in place as a special intern assistant to the police reporter when Jennifer was handpicked by Chicago Day City Editor Leo Stanton to take over the police beat.

"You can dump Block, or you can teach him," Stanton said in his usual blunt fifty-seven-year-old Ivy League way. "Your choice."

"He could probably teach me," Jennifer had said, not kidding. "I'll keep him for now, at least until I learn the ropes."

Stanton had shrugged. "He's an OK kid, a little cocky. Lots of potential. We'll find a spot for him either way. I just don't want you to feel saddled. You've got the budget for part-time help, but you can hire your own if you wish."

Jennifer hadn't wished. At least not at first. There had been many times since then that she would have given anything to have taken Leo up on his offer.

Bobby had been fine the first few days– telling Jennifer where everything was, introducing her to the key contacts in all the precincts. But she sensed something behind his surfacy self-deprecating comments. It wasn't long before she realized that he was working against her.

Bobby Block may have doubted his own worth or ability, but his insecurities surfaced in quiet insubordination. At first, he had simply seemed eager to be in on everything and get his share of good by-lined stories.

But soon Bobby was thwarting Jennifer at every turn, withholding crucial information, leaking her best tips to the competition, and putting her in a bad light before Leo. Bobby wasn't openly hostile until he had gotten her into serious trouble; only then did it hit her that he had been the source of her problems.

In the middle of her coverage of an Internal Affairs Division (IAD) dragnet, Bobby chose to reveal Jennifer's relationship with Police Officer James Purcell, one of the charged officers. Until Purcell was cleared, Jennifer had lost her job– which, of course, had been Bobby's intention.

Months later, when Jennifer graduated to a front-page column, Bobby was so incensed that he took to snooping around her stories, trying to scoop her. That cost him his job, and within hours he was snapped up by the *Trib*, from which he had waged a smear campaign against Jennifer. He even tried to implicate her in a murder that she and Jim Purcell eventually solved.

That cooled Bobby's jets for a while, and except for an occasional veiled barb at Jennifer, Bobby had settled into his role as police reporter at the *Trib*. He had graduated with honors, alienated classmates and profs, annoyed his superiors and coworkers, and raised the hackles of the police officers he needed as sources. Yet still he flourished.

His secret was good writing laced with sarcasm and satire. The readers loved it. But Bobby had a growing list of professional enemies who soon realized that little he had ever said about Jennifer Grey had been true.

Jennifer, however, had been left with a nagging conscience over her failure to ever get next to Bobby– to find out what it was that made him so obnoxious, so committed to making waves, so unhappy unless he was fighting. She felt she and Jim had something to offer Bobby. But she realized she had been naive to think he would listen.

Twice she had called for appointments with him, hoping to bury the hatchet, to just chat, to grab a bite at Berghoffs. Neither time did Bobby even return her call. She had settled on what she would say, how she would begin. It wouldn't be that difficult, because she had grown to appreciate certain aspects of his writing.

She knew he was a better pure writer than she was, with less warmth and feeling and people-orientation perhaps, but with a certain concise purity nonetheless. And he had become a careful researcher. That surprised her. More than a few times she had recognized in his stories much careful homework and documentation of facts.

That was something she had tried to teach him over and over, yet he had been content to wing it, to guess, to assume. Maybe now that he was on his own at one of the top papers in the country, he felt forced to do it right. Or maybe someone was doing it for him.

Regardless, his writing had improved. She wanted to tell him that. But for a long time, Bobby pretended she didn't exist. She decided a cold war was better than his allout efforts to ruin her had been in the past. Jennifer wished he would at least respond somehow, even if to say no to her invitation to lunch.

And then on Wednesday, his note had come. It read simply:

Boy, Jennifer, do I ever need to talk to you!
Yes, let's do lunch this week. So much to make you understand.

B.B.

Jennifer called him right away and left a message for him to phone her. The next day she stood watching the Associated Press wire machine, looking for a Sunday column idea. Often the reporters resented the privileged columnists leaving their offices and getting in the way, so she was careful to stand aside any time anyone approached the machine.

"Hey, Jenn!" rewrite man Dick Harlan called from his desk, phone to his ear. "You know Block from the *Trib?*"

Several others looked up, annoyed, so Jennifer just nodded and approached Dick, assuming Bobby had finally returned her call.

"Found him dead," Harlan said.

Jennifer froze while others gathered around Harlan. "Just a minute," he said, listening. He hung up. Jennifer couldn't make her legs carry her farther, but she could hear Dick from where she stood.

"Didn't show up for work this morning, but nobody from the *Trib* checked until about noon. They couldn't get an answer, and the landlord said his car was still in the parking garage, so someone went over. His girlfriend had just shown up with the same idea when they got there. She had a key."

"How'd he die?" someone asked.

"Nobody knows yet. He do dope, Jenn?"

She shook her head, still rooted to her spot.

"We'll know soon," Harlan said. "In time for the fourth edition."

Jennifer walked stiff-legged back to her office. She phoned Jim. "I just heard about it," he said. "I don't know any more'n you do. You going over there?"

"Is there anything to see?"

"I s'pose. They just found him. Probably haven't even removed the body yet."

"I guess I will. Jim, this is doing a strange thing to me. I don't know why."

"It's always tough when you've known someone, Jennifer."

"I guess. See you later?"

"We hadn't planned anything tonight. You need to see me?"

"Maybe."

"Should I stay available?"

"Would you?"

"For you? I"ll be here."

Jennifer fought tears in the car, wondering if it was because of some strange grief over Bobby Block and the frustration of likely never finding out what he wanted to tell her or the gratitude she felt for being loved by someone like Jim. Who knew what Jim might have had planned for tonight? The baseball season had just started; the Sox would be on television. He often had friends in to watch the game.

At Bobby Block's apartment a few blocks away, Jennifer slipped past police lines without a hitch. It had been many months since she'd had to show her press credentials to get in to a crime scene. She nodded to several acquaintances, none of whom spoke.

She had seen Bobby's girl, still a student at Northwestern, only once before. Jennifer almost didn't recognize her in her grubbies, but Adrienne Eden could have been Bobby's sister. Like him, she was taller and heftier than average.

In jeans and a baggy flannel shirt, her long, curly, black hair a mess, Adrienne sat at the end of the hall, pressing wads of tissue paper to her eyes as reporters crowded around her. Jennifer decided not to intrude just then. But when she turned to check out the apartment, Adrienne cursed her in a sob.

"Wonder if you were here earlier today!" she added. "Little Miss Righteousness!"

Jennifer flushed and ducked into the apartment, wondering if Adrienne could have known about Bobby's note and also realizing that if the other reporters had not known whom Adrienne was addressing, Adrienne would tell them. And now Jennifer found herself not ten feet from the bloated, discolored body of Robert A. Block, twenty-five, deceased. He was bare-chested and barefoot, wearing pajama bottoms. Police evidence technicians shot their final photographs, and the Cook County coroner made a few more notes before signaling paramedics to cover the body and lift it onto a litter.

The medical examiner was taken aback when Jennifer asked what he thought, because she was the only reporter in the room and didn't even have her notebook out. Dr. Jacob Steinmetz recognized her, though.

"Hard to say yet, Miss Grey. Didn't appear to be strangulation, and I found no preliminary signs of poisoning, though he apparently died while eating."

Jennifer peered past him into the kitchenette where a cold breakfast remained on the table.

"Could have been a heart attack. He carried a lot of weight for a young man."

"He couldn't have been murdered?"

"I couldn't say. Don't think so. No sign of foul play. If it was a poisoning, it was pretty sophisticated. Nothing common anyway. I thought he had choked on food, but I was wrong. You can see from the upended chair in there that he apparently bolted from the table into here and collapsed. Nasty head wound from hitting the floor, but I don't think that killed him. I'm guessing he was dead before he hit the floor. We'll see. If this had happened a few years ago, I'd fear cyanide– but I doubt it here."

Other reporters were crowding around. "I"ll have a statement in a few hours," Dr. Steinmetz said. "Nothing now, thank you."

Several grumbled about his having talked to a columnist, but none followed him when he left. "Why does his girl friend hate you?" someone asked.

"I don't know," Jennifer said, wishing she could give them a "No comment" but knowing how they would despise it. "I hardly know the woman."

"She says you had it in for Block."

It wasn't a question, so Jennifer didn't respond.

"That true?" someone asked.

"Of course not."

"Had you two dated?"

"Don't be silly," Jennifer said. "Bobby had worked for me. You know that. I have nothing more to say."

"He was pretty tough on you in the paper. You fire him?"

"No."

"Who did?"

"My boss. I'm through talking."

"Why was he fired?"

"Ask my boss." Jennifer pushed her way through to the elevator. The questions continued until she was in her car, and she sensed the frustration of people who were subjected to that regularly. Her one consolation was that none of the three papers in Chicago was a scandal sheet. The reporters asked tough questions to elicit answers, but none would print the screaming headlines of the yellow journalist.

Was Bobby going to apologize for having caused Jennifer so much trouble? Was he going to explain himself, maybe make excuses? Did he know his life was in danger? Jennifer knew she would never know unless she searched for the answers herself.

Back at her office, she phoned the precinct station house to find that a Cap Duffy had been assigned to the case. She didn't recognize the name. "That a nickname?" she asked.

"I dunno," the desk sergeant said. "Prob'ly."

"Rank?"

"Just a detective."

"Homicide?"

"Yeah."

"Who decided this was a homicide?"

"Who's askin', lady? Young, healthy guy croaks at breakfast with no food in his throat. That sounds suspicious to me, homicide or not. We got to check out the suspicious deaths, right? So who would you put on a suspicious death, someone in vice control?"

Jennifer buzzed Dick Harlan.

"Rewrite."

"Yeah, Dick, Jennifer. Who've you got on the Block death? I didn't see anybody over there."

"I don't know if anybody's on it yet, Jenn. What were you doing there?"

"I have no restrictions."

"I know, but you wouldn't write about that death, would you?"

"I might. Why not?"

"Well, I mean, I don't know. Just seems sorta tacky, that's all. Forget it, what do I know? You want me to let you know when I find out who Leo assigns?"

"Nah, thanks. I'll ask him."

"It'll be a tough one to assign, won't it, Jenn?"

"How's that?"

"Just for fairness, we should find someone who didn't go to Medill, shouldn't we?"

"I guess," Jennifer said.

"That won't be easy around here."

"I didn't go to Medill."

"Yeah, but you're a star. And talk about fairness. No way you'll get assigned to this one. If you cover Bobby Block's death, you'll be doing it in your column, not in the news."

# Two

"So, what did Leo say?" Jim asked at dinner, reaching for Jennifer's hand across the table.

"He agreed with Harlan."

"How about you? Don't you agree with Harlan?"

"Of course. But Leo says old man Cooper doesn't want me to deal with it even in my column, and there weren't supposed to be any limitations on my column."

Jim smiled and straightened as the waiter arrived, and Jennifer watched as he ordered. She had always envied Jim's ability to chat casually with perfect strangers. Usually his rosy complexion and pale blue eyes, offset by almost white blond hair, distracted listeners long enough for him to put them at ease.

When they were alone again, she interrupted her own story to thank Jim again for changing his plans for her.

He brushed it off. "I'd rather be with you than a bunch of divorced cops or married ones who should be home with their wives, anyway. And it's not like you haven't done the same for me."

"But you enjoy relaxing and watching a ball game."

"More than being with you? Someday I'll prove you wrong about that."

Jennifer didn't want to pursue that statement. If they were married, she'd watch the games with him, and they'd kill both birds with the same stone. But the mention of marriage was not going to come from her lips first. Maybe he didn't want to marry a widow anyway.

From the look in his eyes she would have guessed that indeed he did, and she couldn't help looking forward to his endearing good-bye. She never liked the thought of being apart from him, yet he was so loving, so gentle with her, embracing her as if she were a fragile china doll.

He lit old fires in her, yet he didn't push her, didn't exhibit the urgency that would have scared her off. She found him exciting; she loved him. And she couldn't shake the crazy feeling that, though the good-bye would mean she would be apart from him again, she longed for the thrill, the beauty, the purity of it.

After their salads came and they had prayed, she asked, "Do you think Max Cooper has a right to renege on his commitment to my freedom with the column?"

"Absolutely," Jim said, without hesitation.

It had been a rhetorical question, begging an answer that would allow Jennifer's soliloquy to masquerade as dialogue. Jim's response, of course, brought her up short.

"You do?"

"Of course. You believe in freedom of the press, don't you?"

"Ah, yes. But, uh, that was going to be my argument, Sweetheart. How does freedom of the press justify Cooper's position and not mine?"

"Freedom of the press belongs to the one who owns the press, not to the ones who are employed by him."

She sat silent. "But he promised," she said finally.

"That's his problem. He'll have to live with that. But certainly it's his prerogative to change his mind. And he does have a point in this case, Jenn."

"I was afraid you were going to get around to that," she said smiling. "I hate logic."

They ate in silence, occasionally gazing deep into each other's eyes. Jennifer wondered at herself and how she could unabashedly stare at Jim without even attempting to hide her pleasure in him. The April 21 evening was unseasonably warm, so after dinner they walked to the Oak Street Beach and sat on concrete benches.

"I shouldn't have reacted so impulsively to your question," Jim said, his arm around her waist. "You wanted an ear; I gave you a mouth."

"But you were right, Jim. It's just that I want to write about Bobby Block."

"Why?"

"I haven't thought that through. As soon as I was over the initial shock, I knew I had to get to know him as soon as possible. The sooner he's in the ground, the less chance that I'll know anything about him."

Jim squinted out at a blinking light a mile off the shore. "Are you sure there's anything there to know?" he asked. "Could it be that Block was just one of those selfish types who crash through life, destroying everything and everybody in their way?"

"Maybe."

"But it's not his death you want to write about?"

"Not really. There was a core of something there, something deeper than what everyone saw. It's what made him a decent police reporter after all, in spite of everything."

"Decency from indecency, huh? But you can't write about him, Jenn."

"Why not?"

"The guy in the city room— "

"Harlan?"

"Yeah, he's right. It would be tacky. If you're not investigating the death, you can only write about what you know. You haven't talked with the man for months. The only contact you had with him was unpleasant. He was a scoundrel. He was out to get you. He hurt you, slowed your career, never gave you a chance to fight back or even know what his beef was. Is that what you want to print about a dead man?"

Jennifer stood and faced Lake Shore Drive, watching the cars and buses and hearing the tires and horns. After two years of working in the city, those sounds had become a mere backdrop that no longer abused the senses.

Why did she want to pursue Bobby Block to his grave? Should she feel guilty for not having told him of her faith? She couldn't remember one opportunity. It seemed all she had done in his presence was defend herself or be careful not to implicate herself.

That wasn't it. In fact, Bobby knew where she stood and taunted her for it. It appeared to make him hostile, or threaten him somehow. She had tried not to intentionally turn him off. But he had been turned off anyway.

Jim stood behind her and massaged her shoulders. He said nothing. That was one of the reasons she loved him so. He knew when to counsel, when to talk, when to ask, when to be quiet.

"I know there's nothing I can write about him yet," she admitted. Jim rested his chin on her shoulder from behind so he could hear her over the din of the traffic. She turned and kissed him, and they walked back to his car.

Instead of letting him open the door for her, however, she leaned back against it and gently drew him to herself.

"How about two good-byes tonight?" she asked. He raised his eyebrows. "Hmm?"

"One now and one at the door," she said.

"Twist my arm," he said, kissing her.


"I've got a couple of drawers worth of research on some interesting columns," she said in the car. "I'm going to try to bang out three tomorrow before two o'clock. That'll give me a few days to snoop around."

"Where are you going to snoop?"

"Northwestern."

"Yeah?" he said, as if making a list and waiting for the next location. "And Bobby's apartment building."

"Yeah, OK, that"ll be picked over pretty good by the time you get there."

"His family."

"Good. And?"

"And?"

"You're leaving out two perfectly logical places."

"I told you– "

"I know, you hate logic. But you're still logical, so where else will you dig?"

"The *Trib*."

"I love it."

"Why?" "I knew you'd say the '*Trib*, but think about it. Think how you'd respond if reporters from the Sun Times waltzed over to research in *your* shop. How would they be received?"

"It wouldn't be a problem, Jim. It really wouldn't. In fact, I think we'd respect them and show them deference. It would be a good chance to show professionalism."

"Except that you aren't just a reporter, Jenn. And you're not just *any* columnist You're Block's former boss. You're one of the reasons he was fired. You and he go back a long, shabby way."

"Meaning?"

"You had a motive to murder the man, Jenn."

"Come on, Jim."

"I know, but am I wrong?" Jennifer stared straight ahead, as if studying the road as Jim pulled into the parking garage beneath her building.

"I don't suppose they'd welcome me with open arms. So what's the other logical place I left out?"

"It's so obvious I'll spare you the embarrassment of telling you."

"You mean the Police Department?"

"Of course," Jim said.

"Well, sure, that's why I didn't mention it." They laughed.

On the elevator she asked Jim about the detective with the funny name.

"Yeah, I like Duffy a lot. We were uniformed beat cops together. I rode with him a few times. All he's ever wanted to be in his life was a detective."

"And he's a good one?"

"Oh, yes. One of the best."

"But he's not a sergeant or anything like that?"

"Doesn't want to be. Wants to be on the street-hustling, working."

"Will I like him?"

"Oh, sure. Question is, will he like you?"

Jennifer leaned back against her door and took Jim's hands in hers. "How could anybody not like me?" she asked, smiling.

He chuckled. "Cap has never been comfortable around women."

"Is he married?"

"Yes, and to the perfect match. He treats her like a queen, and apparently she doesn't grouse about his crazy hours and his idiosyncrasies."

"Which are?"

"Just like any career detective. He's always on a case. Any time of the day or night, talking about it, making calls, running here and there."

"A woman would really have to trust a man like that."

"Oh, and she does. When you meet him, you'll know he's trustworthy. It's written all over him."

"Children?"

"Nope."

"Interesting."

"That he is."

"Would he be working tonight?"

"Probably. Until he knows how Block died. Why?"

"Then I'm still working."

"Jenn, you're tired. You're not really going out again tonight, are you?"

"No, but I can call him, can't I?"

"Incurable," Jim said, shaking his head. And he kissed her good night a second time. Maybe next time, she decided, she'd try for three good-byes.


"Chicago Police."

"Detective Duffy, please."

"Who may I say is calling?"

"Jennifer Grey, *Chicago Day.* "

"Oh, hi, Miss Grey. Cap's on the street. Want me to have him call you?"

She gave him her private number at the *Day.* Then she called the night wire editor and asked if he would program the phone in Jennifer's office to ring at her apartment number, which Jennifer never publicized to outsiders.

She was nearly asleep an hour later when her phone rang.

"Jennifer Grey?"

"Who's calling, please?" she said.

"Duffy."

"Oh, yes! Mr. Duffy, how are you?"

"I'm, uh, fine, ma'am. How are you?"

"Fine, fine. Can we get together?"

"I don't think so. What can I do for you?"

"I'm calling regarding Robert Block. Have you determined the cause of death?"

"Well, that's not for me to determine, ma'am. That's up to the– "

"I know, Mr. Duffy. Has the medical examiner determined the cause of death?"

"Momentarily."

"Pardon me?"

"I'm calling from his office. We're expecting his statement any minute."
"Would you mind very much calling me with it?"

"Well, I don't know. If it's what I think it's going to be, I may be pretty busy."

"Keeping track of suspects?"

"Ma'am?"

"You know what I mean, Detective Duffy. The only thing you think it could be that would keep you busy would be murder. Why are you thinking it might be murder?"

"Well, not specifically murder."

"What else would concern you?"

"Well, manslaughter, justifiable homicide, stuff like that."

"But you're saying that you think it's probably a suspicious death, so– "

"Well, any death is suspicious until it's explained."

"I know, I know," Jennifer said, exasperated. Maybe Duffy was more charming in person. "Can you tell me why you it might be a death of other than natural causes?"

"You mean besides the fact that the man was only twenty-five years old?"

"Yes."

"No."

"No?"

"No."

"Why not?"

"Because I'm afraid you would be one of the suspects, ma'am, and frankly, you're the only one who's tried to reach *me* tonight."

Jennifer smiled, but kept from laughing. "I imagine I am," she said. "Can you tell me the approximate time of death?"

"Not until I get your alibis, ma'am."

"Uh-huh. And I don't suppose you want those by phone."

"Not unless you want to give them to me."

"No," she said, not wanting to miss the privilege of meeting this man. "When and if the M.E. decides the cause of death, you know where to find me. But let me get a good night's sleep first, OK?"

"You won't be going anywhere?"

"Of course not."

"I may regret it, but I'm going to believe you, because you're such a visible person."

"Thank you."

"And because you're a friend of Jim Purcell."

"That's the real reason you trust me, isn't it?"

"Yes, ma'am," Duffy said, almost apologetically.

"He's the best credential I've got, even with my picture on the front page of the paper everyday."

"Yes, ma'am."

"Tell me something. Block died this morning while eating breakfast, right?"

"I'd rather interview you before we get into that, ma'am."

"I was there, Mr. Duffy. I saw him in his pajamas."

"Alive?"

"Of course not."

"But we might have found your prints in the apartment?"

"I'm not that careless after all these years. No, if you found unidentified prints in the apartment, unless they were on the arm of the medical examiner's coat, they aren't mine. You'll call me in the morning?"

"Yes, ma'am."

# Three

The next morning on her way to work, Jennifer heard a radio report from Coroner Steinmetz. He had determined the cause of Bobby's death as a slow, timed poison that could have entered the bloodstream as early as eighteen to twenty-four hours before he died.

In her office, Jennifer felt strangely distracted as she hunched over a two drawer file and studied research on the three columns she hoped to finish by mid-afternoon.

This was the second time in her brief career with the *Day* that she'd been a possible suspect in a murder case– someone who had been in close enough proximity to the victim that she could not be ruled out without at least a hasty investigation.

Jennifer sensed someone in the doorway of her office and looked up into the wlyly smiling face of City Editor Leo Stanton. He had his usual early morning look. Brown wing-tipped shoes, cuffed and pleated and perfectly seamed dark brown wool slacks, powder blue button-down shirt already unbuttoned at the neck with a slightly loosened blue and brown club tie of just the right width, and an unbuttoned, beige sweater vest.

Leo was classic, natty-but-casual East Coast establishment, and only the ever-present unlit cigar spoiled the effect. He had removed it from his lips so he could grin at Jennifer, but the sight of a well-dressed middle-aged man of success with a soggy cigar in his hand almost made Jennifer gag.

No one who liked the boss ever criticized him for his pacifier, and she liked him. She returned his smile.

"So how's my perennial murder suspect this morning?"

"I'm all right, Leo. How'd you know?"

"You must have your phone turned off or something. A detective has been calling and getting no answer, and he's afraid you've skipped town on him."

"Oh, no," she said, quickly reprogramming her phone.

"Not to worry, Ma Barker. I told him you were here."

"Is he coming?"

"No. Wants you to come there."

"Where's there?"

"Chicago Avenue Precinct Station." Jennifer started to assemble her things. "You've got time," Leo added. "You're supposed to be there at eleven. Anyway, don't I get to hear this story first?"

She pointed to a magazine-stacked chair. Leo lifted the stack and sat, holding the magazines in his lap. "What do you want to hear, Leo? You know I don't kill people."

He put his left hand atop the magzines for balance and returned the stogie to his mouth, jamming it between his teeth and the inside of his cheek so only half of it still showed. It left him remarkably articulate.

"You can't tell me you wouldn't have been tempted a time or two to waste Bobby Block."

"Leo, you know me better than that. I get mad at people, sure, and Bobby drove me crazy. But no, I never once thought of injuring the kid, let alone killing him." She had decided not to tell Leo about the note. At least not yet.

Leo grinned at her.

"You don't believe me?" she said.

"'Course I do. I was just thinking that I often thought of injuring him."

Jennifer fell silent, remembering the storied battles between the undisputed expert veteran of the staff and the know-it-all upstart from Medill who liked to preface his remarks with, "If I was running the city room— "

"Maybe you should be a suspect," Jennifer said finally.

Leo smiled again, then appeared deep in thought, the smile fading. "It's really sad, isn't it?" he said. "I can't say I've missed Block since we let him go, but it's weird to think that he's dead."

"Dead is one thing," Jennifer said. "Poisoned is something else."

"And he had done quite a job for the *Trib*, hadn't he?" Leo said, as if he hadn't heard her.

"You wish you'd kept him and let me go?"

That brought Leo back. He turned to stare at her. "You kidding?"

They each looked down and said nothing. Leo stood and replaced the magazines. A short laugh sneaked from his throat. "Think of where we'd be now," he said. He moved to the door but stopped and turned on his way out. "If you want to talk when you get back, I'll be here."

"Thanks, Leo. I'm going to want to finish a couple of more columns today to give me a little breather."

He squinted at her. "You never needed a breather in your life. What are you up to?"

"I just want time to do my own snooping on this thing."

"Why?"

Jennifer stood and sat atop her cluttered desk. "I don't know, Leo. Block intrigues me somehow. I could never get next to him. You know how you usually know, or think you know, what someone's problem is?"

Leo nodded. "With Bobby, I never knew. I thought I did. I guessed ambition, jealousy, that type of thing."

"Me too," Leo said. "I still think so."

"I don't. There was something more there." She wondered if she would have thought so, had she not received the note.

Leo looked at his watch. "You've got an hour before you have to see the detective," he said. "You got another minute for me?"

He shut the door. This time he put the magazines on the floor and leaned forward as he sat, elbows on his knees, eyes intense. "I've got to admit something to you, Jennifer. It doesn't surprise me that you want to get into this case and probably write about it, am I right?"

She nodded.

"You also know how that would look?"

"I've been told by many people."

"Not by me," he said.

"No, but you're about to tell me I can't do it. "

"Not necessarily. But you're going to have to take a different approach."

"Different from what, Leo? I haven't said anything about how I might do it."

"You forget that I know you, Jenn. If I had to guess, you'd either write about having worked with him and you'd hint about a troubling aspect of his personality, one you admit you have not figured out– "

Jennifer started to speak, but Leo continued, "or you'd write about how shocking and unsetting it is to know someone who has been robbed of life at a prime age. Those are old saws, Jenn, tearjerkers. And it doesn't take a top-notch columnist to do them. They're too easy."

"Well, you don't have to believe me, Leo, but that's not the approach I was going to take."

She told him of her plan to poke around the *Trib*, Block's apartment building, Northwestern, and the Police Department.

Leo shook his head. "Your strength is also your curse, Jenn. You've become too visible to be effective as an investigative reporter. Forget it."

Jennifer wasn't entirely convinced, but she'd heard it so many times she was beginning to waver. "You said you weren't going to tell me I couldn't do it. What's the new approach, the one you think *would work?*"

"You like to write continuing pieces as opposed to one-shot deals like you're trying to bat out today, right?"

She nodded.

"Cover the investigation. You always hear from cops that you learn more about someone's life from studying his death than you'd learn from him when he was alive."

Jennifer thought for a moment. "But that's been overdone too, hasn't it? The highly descriptive pieces about dingy station houses and scruffy cops who work around the clock?"

"So do it fresh," Leo said. "Give it the perspective of a woman who knew the victim. And avoid the cliches. You don't know if this detective is interesting or not."

"Jim thinks he is, but the guy wouldn't win any personality contests, at least based on our phone conversation last night."

"He's got an interesting name," Leo said. "You've got to give him that. Duffy. But why would they put a captain on this investigation?"

"He's not a captain."

"I thought he told me he was Captain Duffy from Homicide."

"No. Cap Duffy. He's not even a sergeant."

"I'm intrigued already. You?"

"I thought Cooper said I couldn't write about Block."

"I've already talked to him about this. You want to do it or not?"

"Of course I do. And thanks, Leo."

"You kickin' me out?"

"Hm?"

"That was a conversation– ending *thanks*, Jenn."

"Since when does the employee kick out the employer, Leo?"

"When the employee becomes as important to the paper as the City Editor, that's when."

"I appreciate that, Leo, but I'm not taking this visible celebrity thing seriously. I know who I am, and you know you're the brains behind my column, so don't think I'll ever get uppity about it. You taught me everything I know and gave me the confidence to do what I'm doing."

Leo stood, smiling a tight-lipped smile. "And don't you forget it," he said. "Seriously, Jennifer, that was nice. Do you really believe that?"

Jennifer grinned mischievously. "No, but it seemed like the right thing to say at the time."

"Ooh, you're bad," Leo said, pointing at her.

She stood and opened the door.

"Now you *are* kicking me out," he said.

"You got that right."

As he passed her she added seriously, "You know what's really good about this? I despise writing timeless columns that could run anytime, even if getting ahead does free me up a little."

"I know what you mean. Your column needs that daily freshness. And if people get hooked on one of your angles, they'll stay with you for a week or even two on the same topic. This should be worth at least that."

At 10:50 A.M. Jennifer announced herself at the desk of the Chicago Avenue Precinct station. She was directed to sit on an oily wood bench across from an identical one, on which was heavily settled an elderly woman, dressed as if for winter.

The woman wore dark, thick horn-rimmed glasses under a heavy scarf tied around her head. She wore a thick overcoat and stumpy rubber boots, flanked on either side by twine-handled shopping bags, both worn thin, but one ironically bearing the name of an exclusive shop in Water Tower Place. Jennifer wondered if the woman had been arrested for shoplifting or was just waiting for someone.

Jennifer tried to smile at the old woman, who stared straight ahead, as if seeing nothing, sleeping with her eyes open. Presently another woman, not as heavy but similarly dressed, trudged from the tile corridor and stood by her.

Without acknowledging her companion's presence, Rubber Boots slowly stood, grasped her bags, and wandered out to the front door with her friend. Jennifer's eyes followed them out, and when she turned back around, a seedy looking man had taken the woman's place on the opposite bench.

Jennifer had planned to kill her waiting time by making up stories about the women and the dastardly thing they might have done to result in their being hauled in by the police. But this man would be even more interesting to use as fiction fodder.

He was reading the racing form on the sports page, and Jennifer wondered if he had ever won a dime. He was thin and small, perhaps wiry, and he appeared down on his luck.

When she was sure he was deep into the fine print, she checked him out carefully. He wore thick-soled, soft fabric shoes; short, dark green, double-knit, polyester slacks that reached the tops of his ankles and revealed thin, light green socks with yellow triangles and elastic tops that had been through a hot dryer one time too many. A dingy dark green and off-white sports coat peeked out from under the bottom of a corduroy car coat, one of those with oblong buttons that poke through any remaining unbroken leatherette loops. It had zippered pockets, one of which still looked zippable.

His face was thin and pointed, and he had a cleft both in his chin and between his nostrils. His lips were a little too generous for his small mouth, and he had large, sad, gray eyes that were slightly bloodshot and peered out at the paper over puffy bags.

He appeared about ten days overdue for a haircut, with curly wisps showing from behind his neck. His sideburns were not only a tad too long, but also curling up in the middle. Jennifer wondered why his hair wasn't greasy, for it didn't seem to fit in with the rest of his appearance. His hands also were clean, and he was clean shaven.

Beside him on the bench was a hat that appeared to match his tie. It was pale green with yellow and brown plaid.

She looked at her watch and decided that if Detective Duffy was on time, she would have about a minute to guess Green and Brown's story. She was daydreaming a tale about his having lost his wallet at the racetrack and having come in to see if anyone had turned it in, when she realized he was looking at her from over the top of his newspaper.

Jennifer quickly looked away and ran her fingers between the back of her neck and her hair. When she stole a glance back at him, he was still looking at her, and she hoped she hadn't offended him by staring at him for so long.

She started to look away again, but she noticed him reach to the inside breast pocket of his sports coat and produce a pair of half glasses. He put them on and began digging through the paper.

She wondered why he needed his glasses to pore through the paper when he hadn't worn them to study the racing charts. He turned to the front page, and she noticed he was reading the *Day*. He folded it up so that her column and her mug shot stared out at him.

Did he recognize her? He looked at the column photo and then at her over the tops of his spectacles. Jennifer couldn't fight a blush as she nodded to acknowledge his gaze. He carefully placed the paper beneath his hat on the bench, ceremoniously took off his glasses, and replaced them in his pocket.

He clapped a palm on each of his knees and leaned forward, peering intently into Jennifer's eyes. "Jennifer Grey?" he asked in an almost sweet, mellow voice that didn't seem to fit.

She nodded again with an apologetic smile.

He reached to shake her hand and she slowly, cautiously complied.

"I'm Cap Duffy," he said, rising.

# Four

Jennifer couldn't suppress an amazed expression, which made Duffy smile. "I'm sorry, but I often do this," he said. "I have trouble meeting people, so I just sit with them and get used to them first."

"Bizarre," she managed, and followed him back to his cubbyhole.

He cleared a place for her to sit, then stepped over her to the rickety chair wedged in behind his desk, which was jammed against one wall. The room was not built for two. "Be glad my partner's off today," Duffy said, then laughed. "Just kidding. I work alone."

"That's unusual, isn't it?"

"Nah. Some of us don't look like cops unless there's two of us. I can pass for anything, right?" Jennifer almost nodded. "But if I'm hangin' around with a guy in a trench coat and gum-soled shoes with a bulge at his hip, then all of a sudden we both might as well be wearin' uniforms, you follow me?"

Duffy wrenched off his car coat without standing and let it drape over the back of his chair. Jennifer did the same. As the detective dug in a file drawer for the case folder, she spoke.

"Forgive my reporter's curiosity. I know why I'm here and that you have a lot of questions to ask me, but could I ask you one first?"

"Sure."

"I'm intrigued by your name."

"Duffy? It's French."

Jennifer laughed.

Duffy straightened up and stared at her, a hint of a smile at his lips. "You got somethin' against the French?" he said.

"No, I was curious about your first name."

"You don't know my first name."

"It's Cap, isn't it?"

"You ever hear anybody go by the name of *Cap?*"

"Well, no, that's why I asked. That *is* your name, isn't it?"

"If you've never heard of anybody going by that name, then it's not my name, is it.?"

"OK," she said,"I'll bite. What's your *real* first name?"

"Would a guy who goes by Cap to hide his real name wanna *tell* his real name?" Duffy was smiling broadly now. "Ah, I never was any good at games. My name is Harold."

"There's nothing wrong with the name Harold."

"I hate it."

"I don't."

"Then you can use it."

"I thought you were supposed to be shy around women."

"Who told you that? I'm not saying I'm not, but who told you? Oh, I know. That big mouth boyfriend of yours."

"So, where'd the name Cap come from?"

"I always wear one, that's all."

Jennifer sat smiling at Cap Duffy. She wanted to ask him if the rest of his ensemble was a put-on as well, but she didn't dare. He could use the clothes as sort of a Columbo facade, hiding the brilliant mind and all that. Then again, he could just be a cop with no sense of fashion.

Duffy suddenly grew serious, acting as if he wished they'd saved the informal banter until she'd been cleared. "I have several questions to ask you, if you don't mind."

"Not at all," she said.

"Do you wish to have a lawyer present?"

"Should l?"

"It's entirely up to you."

"Am I under arrest?"

"No, ma'am. If you were under arrest, I would read you your rights."

"I know. Why did you ask about a lawyer?"

"Just a suggestion."

"Might I be placed under arrest?"

"That's always a possibility. If your answers don't satisfy me or I can't corroborate them, I may be forced to arrest you, yes."

"Do you think it's possible that I murdered Bobby Block?"

"I've learned to never label anything an impossibility, let me put it that way."

"Well, fine then," she said, her heart pounding as she wondered if something in Duffy's investigation had already revealed that she and Block had been trying to get together for some time and that he had, in fact, written to her the day before he died. "Just ask your questions."

"I didn't mean to offend you, Miss Grey."

"Mrs. Grey."

"Excuse me, Mrs. Grey. You're married?" "Widowed."

"I'm sorry."

"So am I."

"Mrs. Grey, I wasn't trying to offend you. I always suggest a lawyer as a courtesy. If I didn't think it was possible you had anything to do with Block's death, I wouldn't have asked you to come here. I'd love to be able to clear you, if for no other reason than to streamline my work. I don't need suspects all over town."

Jennifer was ashamed for having reacted so sharply, but she said nothing.

"Now, if I may begin. How long did you know the deceased?"

"I saw him around, knew who he was, ever since my first week on the staff of the *Day* about two years ago. Then when I was assigned to the police beat about a year ago, I became his supervisor."

"How would you characterize your relationship?"

"Stormy."

Jennifer told him the whole story of Bobby's antagonism, his backstabbing, his deviousness. Duffy made detailed notes in a delicate script as she spoke.

"I know I haven't done myself any good by telling you this," she said, still holding her breath over the note.

"Honesty never hurts."

"Except that if I didn't believe I was supposed to love my enemies and pray for those who despitefully use me, what I just told you might have given me a motive for murder."

Duffy smiled, and it was apparent to Jennifer that, for a moment, his mind was miles away. "Yes," he said absently. "I suppose it might have." His eyes stared past her, and he appeared deep in thought. "Love your enemies, huh?" He smiled again. "That's the Bible, isn't it?"

She nodded, not wanting to bring him back from this strange reverie. "That was a memory verse we had to learn in Vacation Bible school," he said. "Thirty years ago." He grunted as if remembering the good old days.

Jennifer wanted to press, to find out if he was a Christian, but she decided this wasn't the time.

"You believe that, Mrs. Grey?"

"Yes."

"That's good. That's no defense, but that's good. I believe you."

"You believe I'm innocent?"

"Well, no, it's a little early for that. I just believe that you believe that you're supposed to love your enemies and pray for them. Whether you practiced that with Robert Block, I'm not sure yet. Can you tell me your general whereabouts beginning Tuesday at the end of your workday?"

"Sure. I worked a little late finishing up my column for Wednesday. Then I had to hurry home because I entertained my parents from Rockford and Jim, and I was expecting them at seven."

"You say that as if they didn't show up at seven."

"Well, they didn't. I did some fast grocery shopping, and by the time I got home just before six-thirty they were all already there and waiting in the hall. I was going to throw on some steaks and toss a salad, but my father insisted on taking us to dinner at Carson's."

"And then?"

"Back to my place for dessert."

"And they left when?"

"About eleven."

"And you didn't leave your apartment until the next morning when you left for work?"

"Correct."

"Do you remember Wednesday?"

"Of course; what do you mean?"

"The details. Where you went during the workday, that type of thing."

"I spent the morning on the phone with the mayor's press secretary, explaining why I had never written a column on the mayor and warning that if I'd write one, it might be critical."

"This is off the subject, Mrs. Grey, but I'm curious. Why might it be critical?"

"No reason. I have nothing against the mayor. That's why I've never written a column about the mayor. But if I wrote one now, it would have to be about a press secretary who seeks favorable publicity."

"That *is* kinda base, isn't it?"

Jennifer nodded. "I went to lunch with Max Cooper and Leo Stanton at Hunan's."

"And they are?"

"Cooper is the publisher of the *Day,* and Stanton is my boss, the City Editor."

"No, I know. I mean, who are the Hunans?"

"That's a Chinese restaurant. The House of Hunan, Michigan Avenue."

"Good?"

"Great."

"OK, after that."

"Ah, let's see. Oh, yes. I went to Cabrini-Green where I talked with a Miss Hawkins about an opinion piece she had had printed in *Time* magazine. Made a good Friday column. You've seen it."

"Excuse me?"

"You may not have read it, but that's what you were looking at when you were pretending to be someone else out there."

"I wasn't pretending. I– "

"Whatever. You might want to read it"

"I probably will. How long were you with this Hawkins woman?"

"About three hours, until four o'clock."

"All that time for that short column?"

"You did read it!"

"Of course. It takes that long to get column material?"

"Sometimes more, sometimes less. There has to be more than you see in the paper everyday."

"I guess."

"Then I went back to the office for a few minutes, then home to get ready for prayer meeting."

"Prayer meeting?"

"Yes, Jim and I go together whenever he's off on Wednesday nights." She felt guilty now, because it was while she was back in the office for those few minutes that she had received the note from Bobby. She wondered how long she could go on telling Cap Duffy about loving her enemies and going to prayer meetings when she was withholding evidence in a murder case.

"And where is this?"

"At his church in Waukegan."

"Uh-huh. Prayer meeting. And then?"

"Out for a snack with another couple, the Barbers, and then home."

"He stay with you?"

"Excuse me?"

"Purcell stay with you?"

"Never."

"Never?"

"No, sir. We"ll have plenty of time together someday. Please don't tell him I said that."

Duffy grinned. "And you were in all night until work the next morning?" Jennifer nodded. "And then I was in the newsroom after lunch when I heard about Bobby."

"And you weren't gone from the office Thursday morning before that?"

"No."

"Went straight to work?"

"Yes."

"Out for lunch?"

"No, someone went for sandwiches."

"When was the last time you saw Bobby Block alive?"

"I saw him in January at a Chicago Press Club luncheon."

"Talk to him?"

"Tried to."

"Said hi and got no response?"

"Not even that much. I waved to him from across the room. He didn't acknowledge me. I moved toward him, and he moved away."

"That the last time?"

"I think so. No, I saw him at a Police Department press conference about a month later. Just from a distance. No contact" She pressed her lips together. News of the note was ready to burst from her, but she decided to hold it as long as she could. She didn't know why. It wasn't to protect herself. She knew better than that. It was just that this part of it was hers. It was the reason she wanted to investigate Bobby's death for herself.

Duffy sat staring at her. "I have a lot of people to talk to before I clear you," he said. He began reading from his list. "Your parents, Jim, the mayor's press secretary, Cooper and/or Stanton, Miss Hawkins, the Barbers, the doorman at your apartment, and the receptionist in your office."

"You have to talk to my parents?"

"Just routine. I do it in such a way that they don't worry."

"I don't suppose I can tail you around on this case for a week's worth of columns until I've been cleared myself."

"You got that right. Anyway, who said you could do that?"

"My boss."

"Don't I have any say in it?"

"Of course."

"I couldn't let you do that."

"Not even for a friend of Jim's?"

"That would my sergeant say?"

"What will *my* boss say? When Bob Greene runs out of column material over at the *Trib*, he writes about what it's like to shave with a razor for the first time at age thirty-five. Don't push me to that kind of fluff. If you're a good cop, it can only be good publicity, right? That's what the cops need right now, just like the mayor."

"Yeah, and I don't even have a press secretary begging for it. Listen, I'll think about it. But meanwhile, you stay outta my hair and stay accessible. I'm hoping for your sake that your story checks out."

"How long will that take?"

"Not long. I've got a lot of other suspects. This guy had very few friends, you know."

"He had a girlfriend."

"How well I know. She's a suspect too."

"Adrienne?"

"Excuse me?"

"Adrienne Eden is a suspect?"

"That's not the name I have down here." He rifled through his notebook. "I'm eager to talk to a Josie Sisk."

"You've got names I haven't got, and I've got names you haven't got. We could be good for each other, Mr. Duffy."

"Call me Cap."

# Five

Back at her office, Jennifer worked on the first of her undated columns, just in case Duffy decided that– even if cleared– he didn't want her dogging his every move during the investigation. He seemed so strange, she couldn't even predict what he would decide when Leo and Max Cooper visited and asked.

"What really frosts my cake," the old publisher said in mock exasperation, "is that every time I turn around, you're a suspect in a murder case!"

"This is only the second time," Jennifer said weakly, sending Cooper into a laughing jag.

"Lemme know when you've been cleared," he said. "Anything we can do for you?"

"I'd like more information about the medical aspects of the death, but I don't want to step on anyone's toes in the newsroom."

Cooper nodded quickly to Leo who called in a secretary outside Jennifer's glassed-in office. "Yes, sir?"

"Stephanie, I want you to get me photocopies of everything we've got on the Block murder so far, and I mean everything. Reporters' notes, articles, sidebars, printed statements, wire copy, stuff from the City News Bureau, everything. Just tell 'em it's for me, and I want it ASAP. OK?"

"Certainly."

"Thanks, Leo," Jennifer said. "And thank you, Mr. Cooper."

"Don't mention it," Leo said. "Just be sure to give credit for anything you use. A hot quote or note from a reporter shows up in your column with no attribution, and we'll both be skinned."

"And rightly so," Cooper added.

"I've got one more big problem," Jennifer said. "I can't concentrate on anything but the murder. If I don't get this general column done and Duffy doesn't let me write about his investigation, I'll have no column for the Sunday edition."

"You want me to pull a few strings at Police Headquarters?" old man Cooper asked. "I hate to do it, but I would."

"No, I hate that type of thing too. The mayor's office tried to do it this morning, asking for a favorable column."

Cooper swore. "You oughta call the scoundrel back and tell 'im you'll think about it if he can get you permission to cover the murder investigation!"

"I'd rather do it without any obligations."

"You wouldn't *have* anyway! All you're tellin' 'im is that you'll think about it! You wouldn't actually do it!"

Jennifer smiled sympathetically, bringing the old timer back to his senses. "Listen to me," he said hoarsely, "goin' on like a senile, old fool. Well, I'll tell ya, Grey, I want a column from you in Sunday's rag as usual. I'd like it to be the first in your series on this murder investigation, but if it can't be, it can't be. If not, you'll have to come up with something else, and if it's not this afternoon, just make the deadline. Got it?"

"Yes, sir."

That was all Jennifer needed to take her mind off any alternative column and dig into the material which was soon delivered by Stephanie. She'd hear from Duffy in time to pull off a last minute column, if necessary. Meanwhile, she had homework to do in case his answer was good news.

After about forty-five minutes of poring over the material, Jennifer tried to get the coroner on the phone. It wasn't easy. He had gone home.

Even at his home number, she had to go through a receptionist and an aide, both of whom were reluctant to believe that she had learned the phone number from the good doctor himself. But she finally got through.

"I'm in the steam room," she heard him shout over a hissing noise. "So I was wrong about the poison, what else is new? You gonna fry me on the front page for it?"

"No," she laughed. "I've missed a few guesses in my day too. Just tell me about it, and I'll never breath a word to anyone that you first thought it wasn't a poisoning."

"Well, Jennifer, the best I can determine, Block was done in by what my toxicological friends call a cumulative poison."

"Which means?"

"Which means that it was basically an irritant which probably entered the body as a liquid."

"But not through the mouth?"

"I was getting to that, but how did you know?"

"Just guessing that an irritant would injure the mouth, and you would have seen evidence of that when you did the preliminary examination of the body yesterday."

"Very good, Jennifer."

"But what do you mean cumulative, Jake? He had to get several doses or something?"

"No. The first dosage could have been enough, but it may have been in such a diluted solution that it would have been absorbed gradually. I suppose it's possible that he received increased dosages and that they finally took their toll, but this appears to me like a whizbang type of reaction to a time bomb sort of poison."

"For which you as yet have no name?"

"That's right. I saw no evidence of alcohol, barbiturates, or anything like that."

"How would a poison like that get into his system?"

"Well, of course, that's not for me to say. I did a quick study of the body to look for hypodermic holes. Just below his right hip there's about a one-inch square area that seems to at one time have been punctured repeatedly. Now he could have sat on something, or it could have been a series of injections, maybe all at once, maybe in his sleep."

"What are you saying?"

"I'm saying I don't know, and I don't want to speculate. I would not term this a suicide by any stretch of the imagination. The man could have been given an injection while he slept, but he would have had to have been a very sound sleeper to sleep through even one such injection, unless a surface anesthetic was applied. I found no evidence of that either."

"Jake, how will you find out just what the substance was and the effect it had?"

Dr. Steinmetz laughed ruefully. "I'm afraid we're already aware of the effect, girl."

"You know what I mean, Jake. What did it actually do to him to kill him?"

"Well, the big job now is left to the serologists. They have to separate the poison from the normal body fluids and purify it so they can fully identify it. Tomorrow a couple of pathology experts and I will be studying the injury the poison inflicted on the tissues of the major vital organs. This poison acted almost as a narcotic when it finally took effect, affecting the organs and resulting in respiratory and circulatory failure. The way he bolted from his chair and likely died before he hit the floor made me expect to find traces of botulin toxin in his mouth."

"That would have killed him that quickly?"

"Oh, yes. The most potent form of bacterial toxin causes acute food poisoning that can kill you if you get it past your lips."

"Could that be caused by bad food?"

"Unlikely. The cases of botulin toxin deaths I've studied have been deliberate poisonings. Every one."

"But there was no trace of that here?"

"No. But the effect was the same. This, based on what I know right now, was a cumulative poison that exploded upon his system when it was ready. And, as I said at the press conference this morning, it could have entered his bloodstream as long as eighteen to twenty-four hours before death."

"Thanks so much for taking time for me, Jake."

"Anytime, Jenn. Remember our bargain. I gave you a lot more than anyone else in town knows by now."

"Only because I tracked you down and caught you after you'd done more examining."

"True, true. But you're still gonna uphold your end, aren't you?"

"Sure. I'm writing the headline right now, Jake. How's this sound: "Coroner Blows Another Diagnosis?"

"Cute, Jennifer. Good-bye."

"You like that?"

"Good-bye, Jennifer."

"It'll be in Sunday's paper."

"Good-bye Jennifer."

"Good-bye, Jake. Thanks again."

She hung up smiling, glad for some comic relief in such a grisly assignment.

Stephanie appeared at the door, and Jennifer waved her in. "There's a Duffy guy in the lobby asking to see you. Should I let him come up? The receptionist says he looks like one of those kooks who likes to get written up in the paper."

*I wish*, Jennifer thought. "Yeah, send him up," she said.

Her lower back tingled as she waited and wondered if she was as excited about being cleared as she was about whether Duffy knew about her note from Bobby. Or whether he would allow her to tag along, regardless.

She hadn't noticed before how smoothly Cap Duffy moved. He switched his hat from one hand to the other as he came through the door, sat without making a sound, crossed his legs, and settled back expectantly.

Jennifer stacked her papers neatly and entwined her fingers atop the desk, leaning forward to give full attention. It seemed to be what Duffy had been waiting for. "I have good news and bad news," he said seriously.

"The good news is I've been cleared," she guessed. "My references were not only able to corroborate my whereabouts, but they also sang my praises so that you wondered why I didn't go into full-time church work."

"Right, Joan of Arc."

"I sometimes wonder that myself."

"The bad news, however– "

"I know," she said. "The bad news is that you don't think you want me along on the investigation."

"Wrong."

"Really? I can?"

"No, you can't. But it's not that I don't think I want you along; I know I don't want you along."

Jennifer looked hurt.

"I didn't mean to be cold about that," he said. "It's just that I know how persistent you newspaper types are, and I needed to be able to shut the door on that little foray into loophole land you just tried to make."

"Pardon me?"

'When you said I didn't think I wanted you to go. That made it sound tentative, as if you still had some say in it, which you don't."

"You're not trying to sound mean?"

"No, ma'am, I'm truly not."

"That's good. I'd hate to be on the other end when you're working at it."

"I'm sorry."

"So am I. Why does this conversation sound familiar?"

"'Cause we had it this morning."

"Aren't you going to miss this, Mr. Duffy?"

"Call me– "

"I'm sorry, Cap. Aren't you going to miss this?"

"Miss what?"

"Our ease of conversation. You've got to admit you don't get much stimulating conversation in a day's work."

"I get more than I want. All I do all day is talk to people."

"But you're not with them long enough to develop a relationship, to be able to volley back and forth with them. C'mon, I know I've quit conniving and gone to begging, but you know you'd enjoy it. I want to know how you work, where you look, what you're after. Most of all, why."

Duffy looked at her with his head cocked, apparently unimpressed. "You really want to get into the why?" he asked, incredulously.

"Sure, what did you think?"

"I figured lots of whats and hows and whos and wheres, if I remember Intro to Journalism one-oh-one."

"You know why is part of all that, Cap."

"Yeah, but not the real why."

"I would want to get into that. It would be a major part of what I'd want to say. Why does a man give himself to the kind of work you do? What motivates him? What keeps him sane? What keeps him straight? What keeps him from becoming a cynic?"

Duffy sat thinking, but Jennifer had not the slightest inkling that she was selling him. "Well, that's encouraging," he said, "but no. You'd want no restrictions, no rules, no letting me see what you write before you print it."

"That's right," she said, almost wishing she didn't have to say it if it was going to determine whether she got to work with him. But she'd never forgive herself if she gave away her integrity and credibility.

"No, I'm afraid you'd put off my best leads, scare them, keep them from talking."

"I'd stay in the car when you talk to people at the *Trib,* if that's what you mean."

"But how about with Adrienne Eden?"

"You didn't even know about Adrienne before I put you onto her," Jennifer said.

"I would've gotten to her. He was two-timing her, after all."

"Really? See, I didn't know that."

"But she's got no love for you."

"OK, I'll stay in the background for that one too. But you'd have to tell me what she says."

"No, you're not going."

"Cap, you'll wish you'd let me."

"I will, huh? Gimme a reason."

"I've given you a bunch."

"Give me one reason that I'll wish I'd let you."

"Because I know lots of stuff and lots of people."

"Like what?"

She told him what she knew about the toxicologists and serologists and pathologists. She spoke quickly and clearly about what she thought they might find and what it would mean. Duffy's wheels were turning. She was giving him so much more than he had learned from the coroner earlier in the day.

He stood and thrust his hands deep into his coat pockets. She knew the time had come. She showed him the note. He read silently, but he took so long she knew he was going over it several times.

"I'm not too thrilled about this," he said without looking up.

"I know, and I'm sorry. And I swear it's the only thing I've held out on you."

He scowled at the note. "You'll be quiet when I'm interviewing people?"

She nodded enthusiastically.

"You won't ask me any questions in front of anyone?"

She shook her head.

"You won't interview my people. You'll stay out of the way when I say to. You'll let me be off-the-record when I say so. You won't call me at home. You'll give me every bit of information you dig up that I haven't come to yet."

She nodded like a little kid who realized her wish had been granted if she'd just agree to all the rules.

"Jim said you'd agree to everything if I held out long enough," he said.

"Ooh, you're kidding," she said. "He told you that?"

"Don't blame him. He talked me into it. I was dead set against it, but stringing you out for all the guarantees was a great idea."

"I'll wring his neck," she said.

"If he takes any heat for this, it's over," Duffy said.

"You two really have me over a barrel, don't you?"

"I'd say so."

"What would you say if I told you I put Jim up to talking you into it?" she said.

"I'd say you were fibbing."

"And you'd be right."

# Six

Cap Duffy was breaking in a brand new unmarked squad car, and he didn't like it. "It looks more like a police car than a patrol car does! Two whip antennas, a spotlight, blackwalled tires, a municipal license number. Why don't we just put a badge decal on the door and a gumball machine on top?"

"I need to tell you something," Jennifer said.

"I know."

"You *know*?"

"Sure I know. You're gonna tell me that the *why* of my detective work isn't as big a reason as the note you got from Block for why you wanted to write about this investigation. That's all right."

"How did you know *that?*"

"A detective has to be a bit of a psychologist, Mrs. Grey."

"Jennifer."

"Thanks, Jennifer. I mean, let's face it. No matter what you had against this guy, you've got to be curious about his death, especially after that note."

"Even about his life, Cap."

'Well, sure, because you never got close, right?"

"Uh-huh. And it doesn't bother you that what makes you tick is not the primary reason behind this?"

"You never said it was. It's not like you lied to me or anything."

"But I never told you that note was the overriding reason."

"You didn't have to, Jennifer. I knew."

"I *will* write about you and why and how you do what you do, of course."

"It won't make much difference to me either way."

"Seriously? Most cops have at least a little ego, don't they?"

"Most have quite a bit of ego. I have an ego too, but it's not satisfied by seeing my name in the paper."

"What satisfies your ego?"

"Knowing I'm doing something that few other people could do, especially shy people."

"You really consider yourself shy?"

"Who would know better than me? I know I die inside when I have to confront people, but I play games, I playact, I overcome the barrier because I force myself. I know I have to, and so I do it, and I get great satisfaction from it."

"And each time it gets easier?"

"It never gets easier. Sometimes it's more difficult. And then I use every part of my being."

"Meaning."

"Sometimes it's my body. I'm in the best shape of any thirty-nine-year-old you know. I can run six miles in thirty minutes, do forty pull-ups, and one hundred push-ups in two minutes. I can lift one and a half times my body weight. Detective work is not all head knowledge and jive talk. When I get into a tight spot, I have more options than most. That's where my ego boost comes from."

"And it wouldn't give you a rush if people knew about that?"

"It embarrasses me a little to even tell you. Nobody else but my wife knows what I go through to stay in shape. Some of the guys are aware of my condition because we play racquetball, but most of the time I hide under the clothes."

"Tell me about the clothes."

"Clothes are irrelevant to me. I don't know or care what most people are wearing."

"But you dress, how should I say it– ?"

"Tacky?"

"You said it, not me."

"I know," he said "Yeah. I do. And I'd like to be able to tell you it's for some strategic reason, but I dress the same way socially and formally. I'll tell you this, though. It works as strategy, because I'm seldom taken for a cop. Cops run the gamut from frumpy, old-fashioned 'Dragnet' TV show type outfits– trench coats, wide-brimmed hats, black shoes, and white socks– to the modern 'Barney Miller' style, like off the cover of *Gentleman's Quarterly*."

"You can't kid me, Cap. You *do* know fashion."

"OK, but I still think it's basically irrelevant, except for the cover it allows me before I have to identify myself. I often get more information when I'm just hanging around someone, before they know who I am, than I do when I'm peppering them with questions."

"Who are we going to pepper with questions this balmy Friday afternoon?"

"Don't start with the *we* business, Jennifer. I'm warning you."

He was only half-kidding.

"Sorry," she said. "Who are *you* going to question?"

"I'm going back to the *Tribune*."

"Which means I have to sit in the car."

"But not for long. I've got a suspect in there who won't quit."

"Seriously? You think it's someone Bobby worked with?"

"Slow down, Brenda Starr," he said, pulling into a parking garage not far from *Tribune* Tower. "Choosing an early suspect is just one of my things. It helps me focus. I hone in, concentrate my energies, believe with everything I have that I've found the murderer, and I don't let up until I'm forced to."

"Guilty until proven innocent, huh?"

"That's right, except– of course– I never put someone in that category without a good reason."

"Was I in that category?"

"Not for a second."

'Who's your mark at the *Trib?"*

"Name's Young. Christopher Young."

"Chris *Young*? He used to be at the *Day!* He's a buddy of Bobby's, one of his very few. Are you sure you've got something on him?"

Duffy flashed her an impatient look. "No, I just don't like tall, skinny guys– so I thought I'd give him some grief."

"I'm sorry," Jennifer said, but not quickly enough. Duffy was out of the car, slamming the door and striding toward the garage elevator.

Chris Young? He'd gotten his start at the *Day*. In fact, hadn't he graduated a few years before Bobby and put in a good word for him with Leo? Chris was with the *Day* for three or four years and developed into a top-notch reporter and writer before landing a plum rewrite job at the *Trib* for excellent money.

Jennifer even vaguely remembered that it may have been Young who put the *Tribune* brass onto Bobby after Bobby had been fired from the *Day*. Chris and Bobby had been inseparable, and she had heard of no rift. But then she never heard much of anything from the *Tribune*.

What could have gone wrong in their relationship?

Duffy was back more quickly than Jennifer expected. "Stood me up," he said, fuming. "That only adds fuel to the fire."

"It doesn't necessarily mean anything," Jennifer said.

"It means he's avoiding me, and when I've got him in my sights, for valid reasons or not, it doesn't look good for him."

"Tell me why his scent is in your nose."

Duffy turned and grinned at her. "If it ain't Ernestine Hemingway! You gonna use that line in your column about ol' Cap Duffy, the bloodhound?"

Jennifer was embarrassed. "You know what I mean. And where are we going now?"

"Northwestern."

Inwardly, Jennifer felt proud of herself that Duffy was sniffing around the same places she would have. As he headed north, she asked again about Chris Young.

"Ah, it's nothing big, really Just something I sensed when we first talked. He couldn't hide his bitterness over certain injustices in Block's life."

"Such as?"

"Such as the fact that Block was two-timing his girlfriend."

"You mean he was dating both this Josie girl you mentioned *and* Adrienne Eden?" Jennifer asked.

"Right. Josie Sisk is a Chicagoan. Eden is still on campus at Northwestern."

"But his buddy wouldn't kill him for that."

"Not as a rule. Unless Young was interested in one of the young ladies."

"Excuse me, Cap, but I don't know how to say this. The word around the *Day* was that Chris Young was more likely interested in the young men than the young ladies."

"Yeah, I heard the gay theory about Young too. So maybe he was interested in Block and was incensed that he was losing him to not just one woman, but two."

"Sounds pretty thin, Cap."

"Maybe, but there's more. I got the impression that Young wanted to take a lot of credit for Block's career."

"And he probably should. I seem to remember Chris got Bobby both his job at the *Day* and at the *Trib*."

'Well, I got that impression too, so I probed a little deeper. I told Young that I saw Block as one of the young stars at the *Trib,* in fact in all of Chicago journalism."

"Did that make him proud?"

"Hardly," Duffy said. "It opened a floodgate. Young burst forth with a lot of spiteful talk about the fact that the public should someday know the truth behind the newspaper writers in this city."

'What did he mean that the behind-the-scenes guys, the rewrite men, are really the writers?"

"I assume."

"He's right, of course, Cap. *Our* rewrite men are chosen for their attitudes. That may be why Chris had to go to the *Trib* to get that kind of a position. He was too well-known at the *Day* as a hothead and a climber."

"Not the best type for a rewrite man?"

"No way. They sit there with earphones clamped to their heads for eight hours, trying to make readable copy out of poor reporting and horrible on-the-scene writing. A guy has to have the heart of a servant and love his work– not to mention his reporters– to be a good rewrite man. You can't buy or make them– They're born."

"In my book, Chris Young ain't one of 'em," Duffy decided.

Jennifer nodded. "He's got the ability. But not the psyche."

Duffy parked in a small lot on the far south side of Northwestern's campus, and they walked through the heart of the beautiful place, heading north. "Who are we looking for– excuse me, who are *you* looking for here?"

The detective dug out his leather notebook and leafed past several pages. "Ed McDevitt," he said carefully. "A sophomore. On the campus newspaper staff. A protege of the great Bobby Block. He's a jock. Almost made the basketball team. Big in intramurals here. Tall, broad, rangy, good-lookin' kid with sandy blond hair. Real heartthrob type. Studying law. My favorite interview."

"Law students?"

"Yeah. They'll tell ya what you're doin' right and wrong, all that. I can usually tell right away if they've got something to hide."

"You have an appointment with this, uh– "

"McDevitt," Dufry said, sneaking a peek at his notes. "No, but he gets out of class in about fifteen minutes, and he should stroll right by here."

They sat on a wood bench behind a hedge and relaxed while Duffy kept an eye out for the big law student. "We talked about your technique, Cap," Jennifer said, "but we still haven't gotten into the why."

"Why do I do it? Why am I a cop? That type of thing?"

"Uh-huh."

"Like most honest cops, I'm on a justice trip, I guess. Growing up I noticed that the biggest and the strongest and the best-looking and the smartest people always got the breaks, and not only that, they got away with everything. Well, I can't be put in any of those classifications, but I can be sure that justice is done."

"But is justice always done?"

"No, 'course not. You mean because of the court system?"

Jennifer nodded.

"I hear you. We catch 'em red-handed, round 'em up, drag 'em to court. But we can't throw 'em in the slam. That's up to the judge, the jury, the court, the state, and the system. And it's too big and overcrowded. That's why you see guilty people go free. And that's why you see cops tempted to carry out justice on the spot and answer questions later. Because they see something bad going down– they themselves, the cops, you understand– are the witnesses. They testify in court, they've got the dude dead to rights, and to save time and money the judge lets the sucker cop a plea, and we've got murderers, rapists, armed robbers, you name it, on the streets with suspended or commuted sentences."

Jennifer looked up from her own notes. "But that's not enough to put you out of the profession?"

"Nah. If we all got discouraged with it, the whole thing would be up for grabs. A few guys get convicted, and we slow the rest down at least, make them hire lawyers and show up for court and post bond and all the rest. We make life tough for 'em anyway. There's some justice in that."

"But not enough, I hear you saying."

"You listen well, lady."

They fell silent and gazed across the campus. Suddenly, Duffy stood and peered through the hedge. He pulled a couple of pictures from his pocket. "I know that's McDevitt," he said, "but who's the girl?"

"Don't ask me," Jennifer said, craning her neck to see. A dreamy giant in a heavy woolen sweater loped down the sidewalk with a cute, little coed on his arm. At least, she looked like a coed.

"Look at this picture," Duffy said, shoving under her nose the likeness of a young woman with long, blond tresses and a short, compact body. "Imagine her with a pageboy haircut and tell me that isn't the girl he's with."

Jennifer compared the picture and the girl on the giant's arm. The couple neared the hedge. "That's her," Jennifer agreed.

"What in the world's he doing with Josie Sisk?" Duffy asked.

# Seven

Duffy motioned to Jennifer to sit back down on the bench. He joined her, deftly pulling a newspaper from his side pocket, so he would appear to have been sitting there reading for some time when the couple walked by.

The move made both Jennifer and Duffy blend into the background. McDevitt and Sisk were about thirty feet past them when Jennifer whispered, "What now?"

"We follow them," Duffy said, rising. Jennifer wondered how Duffy thought he could look inconspicuous on *this* campus.

A hundred yards away McDevitt and Sisk stopped and leaned against the hood of a late model canary Porsche. Duffy sat under a tree and Jennifer wondered what she was supposed to do. She wasn't about to sit on the ground in her dress.

"Just mosey around," Duffy suggested. "If that's Josie's car, she'll be gone soon, and I'll intercept the big guy when he comes back this way."

Jennifer was frustrated but wandered off. In a few minutes Josie Sisk pulled away, and McDevitt started back up the walkway past Duffy. Jennifer headed that way too.

As the lanky student passed the detective, Duffy looked up from his newspaper. "Hey," he called, "aren't you Ed McDevitt?"

McDevitt whirled and glared at him, puzzled, but kept walking.

"The basketball player?" Duffy said. "Played high school ball in, ah, don't tell me, uh– "

"Michigan," McDevitt said, circling back. "Do I know you?"

Duffy looked around to be sure he wasn't creating a scene that would embarrass the big guy, then pulled out his badge and identified himself. "I want to talk to you about Bobby Block for a few minutes. Right here all right?"

"Who's the lady?" McDevitt asked, staring at Jennifer.

"She's with me," Duffy said.

"Uh-*huh*," McDevitt said, winking at her. She glared at him, and he smiled. She didn't. "Let's at least sit down," he suggested, and they found another bench. McDevitt sat in the middlle. "What do you wanna know?" he asked.

"I just need preliminary information, some help," Duffy said.

"That's good," McDevitt said, "because you're out of your jurisdiction, aren't you? And if you made me sit here and talk to you without arresting me or informing me of my rights, I might have you for violating my security against unreasonable search and seizure."

"Oh, give the kid an A on that pop quiz," Duffy said with a grin. "If it ain't Perry Mason!"

McDevitt looked annoyed.

"Hey, just kiddin'," Duffy said. "Seriously, that was an impressive little rundown there for just a sophomore in prelaw."

"So, what else do you know about me?"

"I don't care about you, Ed. May I call you Ed? I care about your old buddy, Robert Block."

"All of a sudden everyone cares about Bobby. I don't remember that many people caring about him when he was alive."

"Only you?"

"A lot of the time only me. And Adrienne. I owed him."

"For what?"

"He took time for me. He talked me out of my major by telling me the odds against graduating high enough in law to get a decent job anywhere, and he said that while the journalism field has been flooded ever since Watergate and all that newspaper glamour, I had a chance if I stuck with it."

"Stuck with him, you mean?"

"Well, sort of, yeah. He taught me a lot of stuff, made me less naive. Pushed me to be tough, assertive, a digger."

"More cynical, Ed?"

"I guess. Especially now."

"Why now?"

"Like I said, everyone is finally interested in a good newspaperman, now that he's gone."

"How do you figure he died, Ed?"

"How should I know? He had plenty of enemies. Cops didn't like him. Criminals didn't like him. Co-workers didn't like him. What can I tell you? There must be a suspect list a mile long."

"Make that an A-plus on the quiz, kid."

Ed McDevitt looked at his watch. "So what do you want from me?" he asked.

Duffy looked him square in the eye. "You really wanna know?"

McDevitt nodded carefully, as if fearing what he was getting into.

"I wanna know what you're doing holding hands and playing kissy-face with one of Block's girlfriends the day after he's found poisoned to death."

McDevitt uncrossed his long legs and stretched them out, crossing them again at the ankles, and folding his arms across his chest. "That make me a suspect?"

"Maybe."

"Then arrest me and charge me. You can't do anything more or less until I'm indicted before a grand jury."

"Oh, give me a break, Ed. You don't want me to do that any more than I do. It'd be a waste of time. I've got solid alibis on you even without your help. Just answer the question and save me a lot of grief."

McDevitt locked into Duffy's gaze. "All right," he said, speaking quickly. "You've done your home work, so I'll give you a few freebies and save you some time. First of all, Josie is my woman and has never been Bobby's. Bobby was engaged to Adrienne, though I don't think they ever got around to making it official with a ring. Bobby would have been a little too cheap for that."

"You telling me Adrienne doesn't think Bobby was seeing Josie on the side?"

"Of course she thinks that, and she was right."

"I'm not following you."

"Bobby saw Josie, OK? It was all right with me. I owed Bobby. Whatever was mine was his."

Jennifer couldn't contain herself. "You've got to be kidding!" she said. McDevitt flinched and Duffy stared her down. "Sorry," she said, putting a finger to her own lips.

"I'm an open-minded guy," McDevitt added. "It didn't really bother me."

"Baloney," Duffy said.

"It *didn't!*"

"Baloney."

"It wasn't a big issue."

"Baloney."

McDevitt appeared as if he knew Duffy had hit a weak spot. "You won't get me to admit it was a problem for me."

"Why?" Duffy pressed. "Because you were so enamored of Block that he was like a cult leader to you? Did he have you under mind control or something? I mean, what sane, healthy American in the twentieth century lets another man share his woman? Sounds a little kinky, man."

McDevitt glared at him.

"You couldn't have liked it, Ed. You may have given in, but you couldn't have liked it."

McDevitt said nothing.

"I'm saying it gave you a motive for murder," Duffy added.

"But you just said you had alibis for me."

"I do, so where am I, Ed? What've I got? Give an old gumshoe a break."

"You're driving at something, Duffy," McDevitt said.

"You're right. You wanna guess?"

"Not particularly."

"You wanna guess, ma'am?" Duffy asked Jennifer, avoiding her name.

"Sure," she said, eliciting another double take from McDevitt. "Ed has himself almost convinced that he didn't mind sharing his woman with Block, and he didn't want to trouble the waters for fear of losing Josie. Down deep, it troubles him greatly that she saw anything at all in a physical specimen as unimpressive as Block and that she would give any other man the time of day, let alone give him anything else. What you have, Ed, is a love-hate relationship with both Bobby *and* Josie."

Duffy fought a grin. McDevitt looked miserable. "Now you've got Josie all to yourself," Duffy said, "but you wonder how long that will last. You're hurt and disappointed, and you feel guilty because the feeling that Josie didn't care for you exclusively is stronger than the grief you feel over the loss of your friend."

McDevitt stared at the ground.

"Do you think you know who killed Bobby?" Jennifer asked.

Ed shook his head.

"Would you have liked to?"

He nodded, grimacing.

"Were you glad to hear about it?"

His shoulders heaved, but he didn't respond. Duffy put a hand gently on his arm– surprising Jennifer– and McDevitt broke down.


"The problem," Duffy said in the car, "is that the man has solid alibis; he couldn't have done it. But he sure had a motive."

"But so did Adrienne," Jennifer said.

"For sure. And if I can somehow eliminate Christopher Young from the list, she becomes prime."

"I hope you can eliminate him."

"Why? You got something in you that wants to see Adrienne Eden sentenced to death? I thought you hardly knew the woman."

"That's not it at all, Cap. Good grief, I don't want to see anyone die, though I share your interest in justice, especially in a murder case."

"You're one of those liberal left-wing news types that doesn't believe in capital punishment though, right?"

"If you've read my column for any length of time, you'd know how wrong you are about that."

"So why are you so eager to see Christopher Young cleared?"

"Because I don't know what I'd do with it in my column if a member of a competing paper's staff was a murderer."

Shocking Jennifer, Cap Duffy suddenly braked and pulled off to the shoulder of the expressway. He shifted into park and let the engine idle. With both hands gripping the wheel he turned to face her.

"I've finally found the chink," he said.

"The chink?"

The chink in your armor. I knew you were too good to be true."

"What are you saying, Cap? Or should I ask, what did *I* say?"

"You just showed your true colors, that's all. Are you saying that your management wouldn't let you cover it in your paper if a competitor was guilty and that they would expect the same courtesy?"

"No, I'm saying I personally would have a problem with it. I wouldn't want to cover it, to deal with it, to write about it."

Duffy shook his head slowly and pulled back out into traffic.

"You're disappointed in me," Jennifer said. "I can see it all over your face."

"I guess I'm just a little surprised, that's all. I was kinda hoping– "

"Hoping what?"

"That you were different, like you seemed."

"That hurts. I'd like to think I'm different from most people in many ways."

"But not when it comes to fairness and objectivity."

He waited for a response, but she couldn't speak.

"What would you want me to do," he said, "if I found out the murderer was a cop? Sweep it under the rug? I've read your columns about *that*, haven't I? I applauded your stand on that, tough as it was. You called for consistency and firmness, quick and decisive justice. Cops were beneficiaries of the public trust, you said."

"You do read my column," she said wondering how he could remember her exact words.

"I read the ones that apply to me. You wanna know if I'm disappointed- yeah, I'm disappointed. I've got a columnist riding around with me, wanting to write about me and what I do. But what you'll write is gonna hinge on just who the murderer is and what walk of life he hails from, not whether or how we catch him-or her."

"I never said that, Cap."

"Well, you sure did!"

"I didn't mean that."

"Just what did you mean when you said you wouldn't be able to handle writing about a murderer who was from your profession, a competitor from another local paper?"

"Well, I didn't mean I actually wouldn't do it."

"But that's what you said."

"It is, isn't it? I'm sorry, because I know better."

"I hope so."

"I do."

"I wonder," Cap said.

"Don't say that. You couldn't hurt me more."

He looked at her with a puzzled look. "You're serious?"

She nodded, almost in tears.

"I really hoped your integrity meant that much to you," he said.

"Tomorrow I'll talk to Adrienne Eden and Christopher Young," Duffy said, parking behind the *Day* building.

"In other words, I won't be in on either of those."

"Probably not," Duffy said. "But you'll be close by, and I'll fill you in."

As Jennifer was opening her door and thanking him for putting up with her for the afternoon, a message crackled over the radio that he should telephone the station. "Ten-four" he said.

Few of the daytime staff were still in the office, so Jennifer let Duffy use Stephanie's phone, then checked her own desk for messages and tidied up her office.

Duffy appeared in the doorway, ashen faced. "You tired?" he asked.

It was a strange question, she decided. "Why?"

"We've got a big night ahead of us, if you're up to it."

Jennifer was baffled. "Well, what's happening, Cap? I'm supposed to meet Jim in about an hour, but if– "

"I'm on my way back to Evanston," he said. "Adrienne Eden was found by her roommate."

"She was found?"

"Dead."

# Eight

As they sped north again, Jennifer told Cap Duffy that she was surprised to see him so affected by someone's death. "I would think you'd get used to murder after a while."

"There are days," he admitted, "when the bodies and crime scenes seem like nothing more than grist for the puzzle mill. On those days, it's just a job. Interesting, but just a task. But it always hits me hard when the victim is someone I've already talked to or someone who's a key to the investigation, as in this case."

Jennifer asked if Adrienne Eden had been a key in the investigation for any other reason than the fact that she knew Bobby was seeing Josie on the side.

"That, and the fact that she had a key to his apartment. A murderer needs motive, means, and opportunity. She had the first and the last. I'm not sure how poison injected into the system would be characteristic of her. She was a communications major, not a biologist."

The radio came alive again, informing Duffy that two eyewitnesses had placed the female in photograph number 08653 in the Block apartment building as late as midnight Wednesday night. Duffy reached into his breast pocket and tossed his whole packet of photographs to Jennifer.

She thumbed through them, pausing at the grisly autopsy photos of Bobby Block. There was McDevitt, Eden, Young, Sisk, and even herself. "The numbers are on the back," Duffy said. "See if Eden is the number he just read off."

"What was the number?"

"Zero-eight-six-five-three."

"How do you remember that?"

"The zero is easy. I pretended it was ten and the rest went down, two evens and two odds, in order."

"Incredible. Nope. That's not Eden's number."

"Is it yours? It better not be– or you and a lot of your friends lied to me."

Jennifer nearly panicked as she flipped her photo over. "Nope, not me either," she said.

"Sisk," he said. She turned over Josie's photo.

"Right," she said quietly.

"Do you realize," he said, "that the woman has had a drastic haircut since Thursday night?"

"And two people place her at the scene of the crime that night?"

"Yup."

"Can I ask you something a little off the subject? Have you been involved in enough autopsies to know how much weight a body should lose during one?"

"Yeah. A body can lose a lot of fluid, but if you're asking about those pictures of Block, they were taken before the autopsy, so he wouldn't have lost much weight there. Why?"

"I must not have been keeping up with him at all. His face seems a lot thinner than the way I remember him."

"Well, he was still a big boy there. I'd guess two hundred twenty-five pounds."

"But when he was at the *Day* he weighed more than two hundred fifty. When I saw him just a couple of months ago, he was as big as ever, so he would have had to have lost all that weight pretty quickly."

"Interesting," Duffy said, "because you know what we found, or I should say, what we didn't find?"

"Hm?"

"Evidence that he had eaten any of that breakfast on his table Thursday morning. It was as if he had fixed it for someone else and was waiting for them."

"Any evidence of Josie Sisk in the place?" Jennifer asked.

"Some unidentified fingerprints that we can perhaps trace to her. She shouldn't be hard to find."

"Have you matched the prints against Adrienne?"

"No, but that won't be too difficult now either, will it?"

Jennifer just stared at Duffy. "If she was murdered by the same *modus operandi*, she's no longer a suspect, is she?"

"As a rule, that's true," Duffy said.

"Who are you leaning toward now, Cap?" Jennifer asked, reorganizing the photos and returning them to him so she could take notes.

"Let's just say I'll be very interested to know if Christopher Young or Josie Sisk were seen in the vicinity of Adrienne's room during the last twenty-four hours."

"How will you find out?"

"There are no shortcuts to that," the detective said. "You just keep knocking on doors, asking questions, showing pictures, and hoping someone will have a good combination of memory and honesty. The honest ones usually can't remember, and the ones who remember will say they don't."

When Duffy and Jennifer arrived at the Northwestern security command post, campus guards and Evanston detectives were talking with Adrienne Eden's roommate, Lisa Johnson, a tiny girl with curly, dark brown hair and huge, square-lensed glasses. "I only roomed with her since January, and I learned to hate her with a passion, but this is horrible! She was lying face dawn at the door when I came back from dinner at five o'clock. She was a terrible person, but I wouldn't have killed her!"

Jennifer followed Duffy to the apartment, where the scene reminded her of Thursday afternoon at Bobby Block's. Jake Steinmetz would not cover this one himself, it being so far north, but Duffy quickly located a coroner's assistant.

"You wouldn't wanna help me with a little pre-autopsy, would you?" he asked.

The doctor glared at him. "You can't touch that body."

"I know," Duffy said, showing his badge. "I just need to know if there are any puncture wounds just below the right hip. It'll aid in the investigation, and I really can't wait until tomorrow."

The doctor pursed his lips and stared, then reached into his bag for a penlight. He draped a sheet over the fully clothed body and moved everyone else from the immediate area. Within minutes, he returned. "Bingo," he said. "About an inch square, maybe ten tiny puncture holes, none of them terribly recent."

"How recent?"

"The freshest could have been twenty-four hours ago."

Jennifer pulled Duffy aside. "What's going on?" she said. "Adrienne seems to have dropped a lot of weight fast too. When I saw her at Bobby's place, she was wearing a baggy top and I didn't notice, but she's lost maybe twenty pounds. What do you make of it?"

"They were both on diets? I don't know, Jennifer. What do you make of it?"

She shrugged. "I'd like to ask the roommate about it."

"I'd better," he said.

When they arrived back at the security office, Lisa Johnson was begging for somewhere else to stay. "I don't even want to go in there to get my things with a murderer on the loose. You've got to help me move! How am I supposed to concentrate on my studies?"

Duffy received permission to question her briefly. He asked about her roommate's weight loss.

"Yeah, it's just been over the last several weeks. I don't know. We never have meals together anyway, but she hasn't eaten a thing between meals like she used to. She never talked about it. She just quit snacking. Still did a lot of grass, though. I figured maybe she got on to some harder stuff and lost her appetite, but I never saw anything around the place."

"How about you?" Duffy said.

"How about me?"

"You do any dope?"

"Just a little grass, a long time ago."

"Nothing harder?"

"Cocaine. Once. Nearly scared me to death."

"Never dropped acid?"

"Never. What do you want from me?"

"Nothing. Thank you."

"I can go?"

"That's up to these gentlemen."

Jennifer and Duffy spent the rest of the evening, until quite late, questioning everyone within a quarter mile radius of the Eden-Johnson room.

Duffy was right. Most people were hostile, not wanting to talk when they found out what had happened. Others were just curious and asked more questions than they answered. Everyone knew Ed McDevitt, but no one had seen him around that area recently.

Everyone knew the Porsche that apparently belonged to his girlfriend, but no one had seen that around lately either.

The first break came just after Jennifer had called Jim to change their plans for the evening. He volunteered to come and help in the canvassing, but Duffy felt it unnecessary.

A senior girl, living alone on the top floor of Adrienne's building, had seen Christopher Young in the library earlier in the day. "It was about four o'clock, and he was talking with a tall, good-looking guy in a sweater, the guy who usually drives around in a yellow Porsche."

Had she seen either of them later? "No."

Had she seen the car that day? "Yes, right here at this building when I returned from the library. That's what struck me as strange, because I had seen the driver someplace else."

"Who was driving the car when you saw it?" Duffy wanted to know.

"I didn't see anyone in the car, but I passed a girl on the stairs, and the next time I looked out, the car was gone."

"Is this the girl?" Duffy asked, showing the photo of Josie Sisk.

"That's her," the senior said. "But that's not her hair. Either that's a wig, or she's had it cut since that picture was taken."

Duffy got the girl to agree to swear to what she had said, in court if necessary. Two others on the same floor corroborated much of her story. Duffy was elated.

"You think Josie could be your murderer?" Jennifer asked.

"I think we've got enough to warrant picking her up and fingerprinting her, don't you?"

Jennifer nodded.

"And if her prints match those found in Block's apartment?"

"Then I'd say the girl is in serious trouble."

The Chicago and Evanston police put out all points bulletins for Josie Sisk. When Duffy and Jennifer reached the city again, a message was waiting for Duffy to call Dr. Steinmetz.

"He's going to tell me that they found a similar patch of injection marks on the second body," he predicted.

He was wrong.

"I know you know all of that, Cap," Jake said. "I'm surprised you didn't ask for a full autopsy right there in the room. There's nothing too surprising to report, but there are two new developments, one of which I can tell you by phone, and the other I'd like to share with you in person."

"I wish you could tell me both by phone, Jake," Duffy said. "I'm about ready to drop."

"Sorry. I'll give you the first half now and the second whenever you say, but not by phone."

"OK, shoot."

"I don't know what this means. You can put it into the hopper and see what comes of it. But we found traces of an appetite suppressant in the tissues of both bodies."

"That significant?"

"You tell me. Could mean that both were on diets, but this suppressant is not available over-the-counter. It's like a hyper pre-sate and is usually administered only by injection, by a physician."

"Would that account for the needle marks?"

"Likely."

"Could the suppressant be lethal?"

"Only in mega-doses, and it would not cause the types of deaths we saw here. Both of these young adults died on what appears to be a timed release basis. If it hadn't happened twice, and if I weren't always hanging around you suspicious homicide types, I'd probably guess that someone blew the injection, gave the patient something other than what he was supposed to. But two? And people who knew each other? And no similar deaths reported? Too coincidental."

"You wanna trade jobs?" Duffy gibed.

"Over my dead bodies," the coroner said.

"Listen, Jake, do I really hafta wait until we can get together on your other tidbit?"

"Afraid so, Cap. I'm sorry. I'm not even sure it's any more significant than what I just gave you, but it just seems important to me to keep it for other than a phone conversation. Indulge me."

"Fair enough, if you'll indulge me."

"Anything."

"I want to bring Jennifer Grey along when you tell me."

"You can bring her around anytime. But seriously, Cap, you'd better get her to agree in advance that she won't print this information unless you or I give her the go-ahead, and even that will hinge on the wishes of the next of kin."

"The next of kin?"

"You heard me."

"You're gonna make me come out to see you tonight, aren't you?"

"No, I wouldn't do that. Really, Cap, it'll wait till morning, and we can meet in my office."

"You're going to be in on a Saturday morning?"

"You're working tomorrow, aren't you, Cap?"

"Well, yeah, but– "

"Well, I'm just as eager to see this thing solved as you are."

Jennifer slept fitfully, in spite of her exhaustion, and she wondered how a mind like Duffy's ever rested. She bet if she called him he'd be up pacing, making notes. But she didn't dare.

Jennifer's mind wandered, raced, slowed, slept, awoke, and thought some more. Did she have to decide between Chris Young, whom she hadn't seen for ages, and Josie Sisk, whom she'd never spoken to? Why would either of them murder both Bobby *and* Adrienne? It didn't make sense. And what was Chris doing talking with Ed after Ed had talked with Cap? Chris had stood up Cap.

At 3:00 A.M. the phone rang, and Jennifer didn't recognize it at first. *Why is that alarm so, loud? Is it really six forty-five already?* When she realized it was the phone, it scared her. She didn't like surprise phone calls.

*Could something have happened to Jim?* "Hello?"

"Jennifer?"

"Jim?"

"No."

"Who's calling please?"

"Don't you recognize my voice? It's an old friend."

"Who's calling please? It's three o'clock in the morning."

"I know, and I'm sorry to bother you, Jennifer. But I have some information that might help you and your detective friend. Can I meet with you without him there?"

"Chris?"

"Yes. Can I?"

"Where?"

"Lincoln Park, tomorrow morning."

"Make it noon and you've got a deal."

"Noon then. But come alone."

# Nine

For the sake of her sanity, Jennifer called Jim and met him for breakfast. She told him everything. Well, almost everything. Everything except the scheduled meeting with Christopher Young.

"What could the coroner possibly have up his sleeve?" she wondered aloud.

"Embalming fluid?" Jim tried.

Jennifer gagged. "You're as morbid as he is. You should have heard what he said to Duffy last night."

"You already told me."

Jennifer rested her head in her hands. "I'm sorry. I'm just exausted. But think of Duffy."

"I'd rather think of you, but, yeah, I know the homicide guys put in some long hours. You can't schedule when the breaks will fall into your lap."

"I get the impression that Duffy makes more breaks than he waits for, though," she said.

"Impressive, huh? Didn't I tell you?"

"You didn't tell me half of what I've discovered in Cap Duffy. Really quite a character."

"I like him," Jim said.

"I'm not sure whether I like him yet," Jennifer said. "But he is interesting. I've already got a couple of columns rattling around in my head, and we've hardly started the investigation."

"Sounds like it's almost over, Jenn. If you can tie Young with Sisk somehow, you've got conspiracy, collusion, whatever you want. And if you can't tie 'em together, one is probably guilty."

"I don't know, Jim. It almost sounds too easy."

"Then make it hard, Jenn. It'll make for a better column."

"Eat your breakfast."

Cap Duffy was stony when Jennifer met him in the downstairs lobby of the building that housed the medical examiner's office. "You wanna talk about it," Jennifer said, "or are you just not a morning person?"

"I'm enough of a morning person," he said. "It's just that very few of the prints we pulled in Block's apartment match with the Eden girl, but plenty of 'em match Sisk."

"That should make you happy. Where'd you find Sisk?"

"That's just it. We didn't. She's blown. McDevitt isn't talking, and I tend to believe he really doesn't know where she is."

"Why is he so believable all of a sudden?"

"Because he gave us several leads on where we might find her. All dead ends so far, but I think he's really trying."

"If she's got his car, she'll be easy to track."

"She doesn't," Duffy said.

"How'd you get the prints if you don't have her?"

"We got a warrant and pulled a set from her apartment, which, by the way, is not too far from Block's. Then we got an old set from the state police. She was kind of a rowdy in high school and got busted a couple times when she was eighteen. Just old enough to make 'em keep her prints on file."

As they sat in Dr. Steinmetz's swank waiting room, Duffy continued. "We also got Sisk's prints from Adrienne's place."

"Doesn't that just about wrap it up, Cap?"

"You'd think so, but it's all circumstantial. Pretty impressive circumstances, I would say, with eyewitnesses placing her at the scenes of the deaths. Notice I didn't say she was placed at the scenes of the *crimes*."

'What's your point?"

"Just that I'm not sure the places where we found Block and Eden dead were the places where the crimes were perpetrated. There's little evidence that Josie was at either place when the victims actually died."

"I can see why you're frustrated."

"That's not all of it. I'm also upset with this crazy Young character. I've got a much better suspect, yet Young chooses to run now. I tried to reach him at his office this morning, and he's on some three-day leave of absence. No one is saying where he went. If he's innocent, what's he running from?"

"Maybe he's involved in the thing with Sisk," Jennifer said.

Duffy apparently didn't want to waste time thinking about it. "Yeah, well, who knows?" he said. "He'd do himself a big favor by sticking around long enough to get cleared."

"If he's innocent, you mean."

Duffy cocked his head and pointed at Jennifer, as if conceding the point. Then they were called into Dr. Steinmetz's office, a beautiful, book-lined, mahogany sanctuary.

"It ain't much, but it's comfortable," Jake deadpanned.

"Yeah," Duffy added, "and paid for."

"That it's not," Steinmetz admitted. "Sit down, please."

They sat at a small antique table near a leather divan. The coroner had the Block file on the table, secured by two large rubber bands he never removed, though he frequently tugged at them and let them slap the manila folder.

"Did you inform Miss Grey that this is off-the-record until we say it isn't?"

Duffy nodded, and they both looked to Jennifer. "If you say it's off-the-record gentlemen, it's off-the-record. I *do* hope you'll cut off the restraint as soon as possible though, whatever the information is."

Steinmetz scowled and stared at his hands, then rose and slowly paced the room, stopping at the ten-foot window casing where he pulled back a heavy, dark drapery and peered out into brilliant sunlight. When he let go of the drape, the room returned to a yellow dullness, illuminated by just two table lamps.

"Well, Cap," Jake said, turning to face him with his hands in his pockets pushing his charcoal three-piece suit coat back, "as I said, I'm not sure of the significance of this, but here goes.

"Remember I told you that a couple of pathologists and I were doing some further work on the Block body the other night?"

Duffy nodded.

"We found something we didn't expect. We found something we couldn't have seen before because we weren't looking for it, and even if we had been, we were looking in the wrong place. The boy had colon cancer, Cap, and I would have given him fewer than six months to live."

Silence hung in the room for several minutes. Finally, Jennifer asked, "How long would he have had it?"

"Could have been a couple of years. It would have had the symptoms of colonitis at first and would have been terribly painful and depressing. The cancer then can be held in check for some time. But once it kicks up again after a brief remission, it's only a matter of time.

"My colleagues agree he was in the last stages of life. It was an ugly mess that would have killed him, even if it hadn't spread too far, which-we discovered-it had."

"Shouldn't you have been able to see that right away?" Cap asked.

"Another medical examiner might have. Then again, there was no reason to examine the colon the first time through. We found what we felt had killed him, and we saved the more careful work for later."

"Are you saying the cancer killed him?" Jennifer said.

"No, no, not at all. Don't misunderstand that. He still had several months, and he had to have known about it. But it was an as yet undetermined poison that shut down his cardiovascular and respiratory systems."

Duffy sat thinking, jotting a few notes in his neat script. No one spoke until he said, just above a whisper, "You wonder if we're looking at a suicide here, don't you, Jake?"

The doctor gave a wan smile. "That's not my department, Cap."

"Sure it is. You're supposed to speculate about the cause of death."

"I can tell you *what* did it, Cap. But when I list 'person or persons unknown,' I mean it. The person could have been Robert Block, but I don't know. I just don't know."

"Suicide crossed your mind?" Jennifer asked.

"I'll admit that."

"How about a double suicide?" Cap suggested, startling Jennifer.

"I thought of that too," Steinmetz said sadly. "He knew, she knew. His death was the trigger. She followed suit. It's possible."

"Yeah, it's possible," Duffy said. "But there are too many other people involved, and too few of them are in the clear yet. I'm still in the chase."

"And well you should be," Jake said. "I just thought you should know."

"I appreciate it, Doc. You know that."

Jennifer fought tears. "I appreciate it too, Jake."

"But you won't print it."

"No, of course not. Someday, maybe. To me it's vindication for Bobby in a way."

"You mean if it was a suicide."

"No, even if it wasn't. It explains him, his temperament, his attitude. It doesn't justify anything. Many people become courageous heroes in their final days, but at least it explains a few things. People, many people, should know that."

"But not now."

"Whenever you say," Jennifer said.


Neither Duffy nor Jennifer spoke as they rode the elevator to the first floor and trudged to the car. In fact, they had ridden around the city for twenty minutes before Jennifer finally asked where they were going. Cap admitted that he hadn't the foggiest idea.

"You got a column to write or anything?"

"Sure, but I don't want to miss anything."

"You won't," he said. "I'm just going back over all my notes and try to piece together the last full day of both victims' lives. I really can't do much now until I find Young or the APB turns up Josie Sisk. And when was the last time you heard of an all points bulletin working as fast as you'd like?"

"Could I watch you recreate the last days by going through your notes?" Jennifer asked.

"I'd really rather you not. It's kind of a silent process, and having to talk my way through it would ruin my concentration. If you don't mind."

"l don't mind," she said, feeling guilty about not telling him about Chris Young. "I should be back at the offIce by eleven-thirty anyway to make a noon appointment."

"You want me to call you if we turn up Sisk?"

"Sure."

"You can break your appointment if necessary?"

"Well, no, if you find her around noon, I"ll just have to catch up with you later."

"You've got an hour," Duffy said. "You wanna get some coffee?"

For some reason, that sounded great to Jennifer. it would take her mind off Bobby's disease and her secret meeting at noon.

In a vinyl and linoleum designed coffee shop at the corner of Clark and Chicago, Jennifer asked Cap if she could ask him something totally unrelated to the case– sort of personal– and would he promise not to be offended or afraid to tell her to mind her own business.

"I'm already dying of curiosity," he said. "Fire away."

"Well, it's just that when we first met, you mentioned that you had been to vacation Bible school as a child."

"Yeah."

"I'm curious about that."

"Oh, it's just a thing that churches have and they invite all the kids from the neighborhood, whether they go to that church or not. I didn't go to the church. In fact, we didn't go to any church except some ethnic orthodox thing on Easter and Christmas. I don't even remember the name of that, but it was huge and scary."

"You talked about vacation Bible school as if you still remembered a lot of it. Did you go every year?"

"No, I only went once. It was a week or so long, and we had fun." For a moment Cap stared out the window at the traffic on Clark Street, but his eyes were unfocused. His speech slowed. He was a child of nine, running up the street to VBS.

"We made stuff," he said. "And there was this guy, Uncle Chuck he called himself. I never saw him before or since, though he came by the house a few times. My father wouldn't let him see me. He said the church had me for a week and almost ruined me for life, and that was all he was going to stand for."

"How did it almost ruin your life?"

"Oh, it didn't really. My dad was just scared. Afraid of the unknown. See, one day I came home saved, and it just about did him in."

"Saved?" Jennifer said, knowing exactly what Cap was talking about but wondering if *he* did.

"Yeah, saved. I was singing all the songs about having met Jesus at the crossroads and choosing to follow Him. I *had* chosen to follow Him too, and I mean I meant it. It was real. Isn't that funny?"

"I don't think it's funny at all, Cap."

"Well, ya know, I didn't either. I was devout for a kid who wasn't allowed to go back to where all the fun and the treats and the kids and the games and the stories were. I kept some of the papers and booklets and stuff and read them until they wore out. I still remember the verses, like the one that came back to me the other day. And I remember the Bible stories too."

"But you never went back to church?"

"Not until I was in the army. I tried a few churches that didn't appeal to me. And when we got married, my wife and I went to the same kind of church that she grew up in. But we just kind of faded away from it. You know, it's a funny thing– "

"What, Cap?"

"I'm glad you asked about that because I don't think I've ever in my whole life told anyone acept my mom and dad about being saved. Not even my wife."

"That's sad."

"Yeah, it kinda is, because it was such a shaping experience for me."

"In what way?"

"I don't know. It made me a different person, it really did. For a long time I prayed to Jesus every day, asking Him what I should do or not do."

"And did He tell you?"

"Well, my conscience sure worked overtime. You know, I grew up in a pretty rough ethnic neighborhood. But after that, I never once got into serious trouble. I never stole anything again, I quit beating up kids, I never skipped school– that was unheard of– and I never smoked or drank. Well, I tried it a couple of times and didn't like it– so I never did it, not even in the service. And, you know, I never was unfaithful to my wife, even before we were married— you know what I mean."

Jennifer nodded. "And you credit that to this experience you had as a child?"

"Oh, I'm sure of it. I wasn't raised by any example of virtue, though my mother was a pretty decent woman. But you know, to this day I don't even lie. I've never cheated on my income tax. I don't take advantage of other people's mistakes that go in my favor."

"All because you were saved?"

"Well, why else?"

"You still pray?"

"No, not really."

"You still believe there's a God who loves you and a Jesus who saved you from your sins?"

"Sort of, yeah, I do. I know that sounds crazy, but there's no logical reason for the basically honest type of person I am. The odds all pointed in the other direction, but something happened to me in vacation Bible school when Uncle Chuck prayed with me."

"Can we talk more about this sometime, Cap?"

"Sure, if you want to. But I don't want any of this in the paper, Jennifer. You understand? None of it. All of this was off-the-record."

# Ten

Jennifer cruised around Lincoln Park until she spotted Chris Young. He was leaning against the front door of his light blue, four-door, Ford Fairmont near a viaduct. His arms were folded across his chest, and his feet were crossed at the ankles. He wore sunglasses and stood so still he could have been asleep.

Jennifer pulled up next to him and rolled down her window, but she said nothing. Because of his dark shades, she couldn't tell if he saw her yet. She was tempted to honk the horn, but she didn't. She just sat there with the engine running.

Finally he grinned a tight-lipped smile and uncrossed his arms and legs. He put both hands atop her car and leaned from the waist to put his face next to hers. "Wanna go for a ride?" he asked.

"Not in your car," she said, amazing herself at her calmness.

"You don't trust me?"

"Should I?"

"What, that detective buddy of yours been filling your pretty little head with stories about the homicidal homosexual?"

"No, but I don't understand why you're avoiding him if you're innocent."

"I just don't need the hassle, Jennifer. Anyway, I wanted to give *you* my information, not him."

"What information?"

"My car or yours?" he asked.

"Not yours."

"You still don't trust me, and I'm doing you this favor?"

She didn't respond.

"All right then, I'll ride with you." He loped around to the other side of his car and pulled a brown paper-wrapped package from the glove compartment, secured with masking tape. Jennifer tried not to let her imagination run wild and decided she wouldn't ask about the package.

He slid into the passenger's seat and smiled at her. She was not about to be pleasant. "Will you take off those ridiculous glasses?" she asked. "It's overcast, for pete's sake!"

He looked disgusted with her but took them off and jammed them into his shirt pocket, pouting. "So where am I supposed to go?" she said.

"Anywhere. Just go up on the Drive, and you can pull off into one of the beach parking areas."

"You'll forgive me if I keep us in plain sight of the Drive."

He shook his head. "You really *are* paranoid, aren't you?"

"Shouldn't I be? Two people have been murdered in apparently bizarre ways, and you and I knew both of them. How do I know you're not going to drag me off somewhere and stick me with a needle and leave me gasping for breath?"

"How do *I* know *you* won't do the same to me? You had more of a motive for killing Bobby than I did."

"*You* afraid of *me*?" she said to the towering Young. "That'll be the day." She pulled off Lake Shore Drive into a parking area. "Now, let's get on with this."

"You in a hurry?"

Jennifer wanted to say yes, because no one knew where she was. But she decided that was just the kind of information Chris shouldn't have.

"I *will* be expected back soon," she said, knowing that at least her boss would wonder where she was.

"Let's take a quick walk, then."

"I'm not taking any quick walk, Chris! Honestly, do you have to be such a grandstander? Tell me whatever you're going to tell me or give me whatever you're going to give me and let me get out of here, OK?"

"OK!" he said, swearing. He shook his head again and turned away from her to stare out the window. "I've got something for you, but I've gotta be like Deep Throat in the Watergate thing."

"You've got to what?" she said, incredulously.

"I've got to remain anonymous. You can't write in your column where you got this stuff. I mean, it'll be obvious you got it from an insider, and you may want to say it was someone from the *Tribune* so people won't think it was from Josie."

"I'll at least be telling Duffy and Jim Purcell," she said.

"No! You can't! Then it's no deal!"

"What's the matter, Chris? You think I'm going to let Cap Duffy waste his time looking for you when there's no need? I'm already going to get royally chewed out for not telling him I was coming to see you."

Young stared at her. "You *really* didn't tell him? I can hardly believe that."

Jennifer could have kicked herself. What she didn't need was to make herself more vulnerable to this character. "No, I didn't. But I'm going to, and you can't stop me."

"Then maybe I won't give you what I was going to give you."

"Suit yourself, Chris," she said. "I'm tired of this game."

"I thought you were a curious reporter-columnist," he tried.

"I am. I'm curious to know if I'm going to survive this crazy meeting."

It was obvious he got great delight in imagining that she was really afraid of him. He could barely contain a smile. "You're really worried, aren't you?"

"Yes, I am. But let me tell you something, Chris. Unless you're armed, you're going to regret it if you try anything with me."

"Oh, excuse me, lady! I'm really scared now! What are you going to do–hit me with your purse?"

"I'm not saying I could defend myself for long, Chris, and you may wind up killing me, but I guarantee you'll regret it."

Young opened his door and staggered from the car, laughing hysterically and banging on the hood. "You're too good!" he shouted gleefully. "You're too funny!"

He had left his package on the seat between them, and when he turned his back to howl into the wind, Jennifer swept it to the floor and beneath her seat. She jumped from the car and smiled at him. "I guess I have been a little silly," she said. "I really don't think you're the murderer, Chris, and I know you wouldn't try to hurt me."

He was still laughing. "Really, Jennifer, what were you going to do to me? When you were really worried about me, I mean?"

She didn't appreciate being laughed at. She reached into her purse and pulled out her key ring, letting a tiny sheath of metal protrude between the ring and middle fingers of her right hand. "I would have used this," she said snapping her wrist and causing the metal to pivot away on its hinge and exposing a two-inch, razor-sharp blade.

Young flinched and stepped back, suddenly sober. "You would have seriously used that on me?" he said.

"If necessary. Of course."

"Well, I don't have, nor did I ever have, any plans to harm you, Jennifer. You should know that."

"Don't make my caution *my* problem, Chris. You're the murder suspect who's eluding the police, not me. I don't think it's so weird for me to be prepared to protect myself."

"So, you trust me enough now to take a little walk?"

"I don't trust you much, but I guess we can walk. Not far though. Not out of sight of the Drive."

As they walked through a small row of trees, he said,"I just want to give you something that belonged to Bobby. But first you have to promise that you won't tell anyone that you got it from me or that you even saw me."

Jennifer just kept walking, her head down, yet always aware of her proximity to Lake Shore Drive, the car, and Chris. When they were about 150 feet from the car, she stopped and looked up at him. "I already told you, I have to tell at least two people that I saw you. I– "

He interrupted with a string of profanities that sent her stomping back toward the car.

He hurried along beside her, berating her, begging her, trying to reason with her. "I can't give you his stuff unless you promise, Jennifer. I haven't even read it, haven't even opened it, so I don't know or care what's in there. I just had a hunch it might help in the investigation, that's all!"

"What do you care about the investigation?" she asked. "You won't even talk to Duffy."

"All right, that's it!" Young said. "Forget it! You're gonna tell him you saw me, but I'll be long gone when he comes looking for me, and I'll burn what I was going to give you!"

"Do whatever you have to do, Chris," Jennifer said.

He hurried ahead of her to the car and opened the passenger door. She prayed he wouldn't look under the seat. He backed out of the car and wailed. "Jennifer! We left the car unlocked! Now where's my package? Someone's stolen it! Jennifer!"

She tried to look concerned and hurried to him. "Where was it?" she asked.

"Right there on the seat!" he said, nearly in tears. "Jennifer, you tricked me! Someone's here! Someone's been watching us! You took the walk so someone could steal my package from the car!"

"How would they know you were going to leave anything in the car, Chris? Don't be ridiculous; there's no one here."

He lunged at her and grabbed her by both lapels, pulling her face up to his. His eyes were wild, and he grimaced as he spoke. "I've got to find that package," he hissed. "Even thinking of giving it to you was a betrayal of my dead friend. It was private! And if you tell *anyone* you saw me, you'll never get it." He began to cry. "Oh, Jennifer, I have to get it back! And you have to promise you won't tell anyone, so I can give it to you."

"Forget it," she said.

His hands slid up to her collar and his palms went to her neck, thumbs in front. She drove her right hand between his arms in an uppercut and stopped with the tip of her small blade resting lightly under his chin. He slowly released his grip on her neck and raised both hands, palms open, fear in his eyes.

She kept the blade under his chin with her right hand and gently guided him back, her left hand slipping a small chemical spray cannister from her pocket. She gave him a miniscule blast of mist in the face and pulled the blade away as he tripped backward over a carstop and sprawled in the gravel at the edge of the lot.

She turned and ran to her car, calling over her shoulder. "You can walk back to Lincoln Park!"

As she pulled away he scrambled to his feet and chased the car. He got close enough to bang both fists on the trunk before he fell face first to the pavement. He made a sickening sight in her rearview mirror, a tall, skinny, miserable excuse for an adult, lying face down, sobbing, and slamming his fists on the pavement.

Jennifer was shaking as she parked behind the *Day* building and reached beneath the seat. For several minutes, she worked at the masking tape on the package until she ruefully realized that the weapon she had so deftly used on Chris Young would also work on his package. It sliced open easily.

Inside she found twelve thin, neatly and alternately stacked reporter's spiral notebooks, the type that fit easily into a suit coat side pocket. Each was marked "Private and Confidential" and bore a sticker that said, "If found, please call Robert Block at the *Chiacgo Tribune* immediately. Reward."

Each was also dated, and a quick leaf through the first notebook, the one that began January 1, showed that Block had learned how to best use the reporter's most valuable tool. Each entry was dated and timed. The interview notes and miscellaneous information had been scribbled almost illegibly, but having worked with him, Jennifer was able to decipher it. Since such information had been ruled admissible in court– in the Watergate hearings– young reporters like Block had learned to protect themselves with meticulous records and direct quotes and research information.

It was a gold mine, Jennifer knew. From the trunk she grabbed the briefcase she seldom used, carefully placed the rewrapped package inside, and locked the latches. When she got to her office, the Saturday secretary, Gail, was waiting with a message for Jennifer to call Duffy at the Chicago Avenue station.

"You wanna talk by phone, or shall I come over there?" Jennifer asked when she reached him. "I've got some exciting stuff for you."

"Likewise," he said. "We've found both Sisk and Young."

"Are you serious?" she asked.

"Course. Sisk wasn't far away and wound up turning herself in. Young was found wandering down Lake Shore Drive, crying and claiming he'd been the victim of a hit and run driver near the beach. What've you got for me?"

Jennifer was laughing so hard she couldn't speak. As she hung up she called out, "Gail! Please call Duffy back and ask him to call me when he's released Young. I'll go see him then."

# Eleven

"Young is a first-class weirdo," Duffy told Jennifer just after three o'clock. "His eyes were bloodshot, and he couldn't quit crying. I still say he had a motive, but his alibis have all checked out since I last talked to him. We had to let him go. I have this nagging suspicion that he knows more than he's letting on, and he keeps saying cryptic things about what you should know."

"What *I* should know?"

"Right."

"Well, I'll fill you in on that after you bring me up to date on Sisk."

"I'll be interviewing her in the interrogation room in a few minutes. You can't be in there, but you can hear and see through a two-way mirror, if you'd like. You can't use anything either of us says in the paper unless you clear it with me, though. Now what have you turned up that's one, so important, and two, so hilarious that you hung up on me?"

But they were interrupted by a message that Miss Sisk was waiting in the interrogation room. Duffy positioned Jennifer where she could see and hear best, then told her to be ready for anything.

"What do you mean by that?"

"I'm gonna push her pretty hard. For one thing, she could be guilty."

"For sure, or is she just the one you're concentrating all your efforts on right now?"

He smiled at her. "Both."

He pulled back a curtain that allowed Jennifer to see clearly into the interrogation room where a matron sat in the corner and Josie Sisk sat on one side of a wood table, smoking idly, but tapping one foot on the floor.

Duffy appeared distracted as he entered the room and didn't look Josie in the eye at first. "Hi, Miss Sisk," he said quickly.

"Ms.," she corrected.

"Hi, *Miss* Sisk," he repeated with emphasis, surprising both Jennifer and the matron and causing Josie to widen her eyes, narrow her mouth, look up and around the room, and nod knowingly, as if she had just fully realized what she had gotten herself into.

"My name is Duffy– "

"I know who you are."

"– and this is Matron Gladys Sprague."

"I know who she is too."

"Well, good. Since you know who everyone is, I want to tell you that we appreciate your turning yourself in and saving us a lot of time, trouble, and expense trying to track you down."

"Don't mention it."

"You have the right to remain silent, Miss Sisk, and I suggest you exercise it." It was the first time Duffy had looked her in the eye. "Anything you say can and will be used against you in a court of law."

"I know my rights. I been busted before. Anyways, how come you're collarin' me when I came in on my own?"

"You have the right to have a lawyer present with you while you are being questioned. If you can't afford one, a lawyer will be appointed for you. Do you understand these rights as I have explained them to you?"

"Yeah, yeah."

"Do you waive the right to a lawyer?"

"I can afford judges– what do I need a lawyer for?"

"Then you're waiving the right to have an attorney present?"

"Yeah!"

"And you're obviously waiving your right to silence."

"Yeah."

"Do you understand that you are being placed under arrest for the murders of Robert Block and Adrienne Eden?"

"Both of 'em?"

"That's correct. Did you murder only one of them?"

"No! I didn't murder nobody! I just didn't know I was gettin' busted for both of 'em."

"Which murder did you think you were under suspicion for?"

"Adrienne."

"Why?"

"Because I was there at her place that day."

"You weren't at Block's before he was killed?"

"Plenty of times. I was s'posed to have breakfast with him that morning. Or at least breakfast at his place. He wasn't eatin'."

"Why not?"

"Who knows? He quit eatin' a couple months ago."

"Why didn't you show up?"

"For breakfast?"

"Uh-huh."

"He called and tol' me Adrienne was coming over."

"What time was this?"

"About seven-thirty I guess, quarter to eight."

"When were you supposed to have been there?"

"About eight-thirty."

"Why couldn't you be there if Adrienne was there?"

"What are you, crazy or somethin? Adrienne didn't know about Bobby and me."

"Can I ask you a personal question, Miss Sisk?"

"You already have. Lots of 'em."

"I want to ask one more, and I don't mean to offend you."

"You're trying to get me on two murders I didn't do, and you don't want to offend me?"

"Miss Sisk, how did you get next to two reasonably intelligent men when you sound so stupid?"

She glared at him. "What're you sayin?"

"I'm saying I don't understand how a newspaperman– a graduate of Medill School of Journalism– and another journalism student at the same respected university could see anything in a mush-mouth, uneducated type like you. Nothing personal."

It was all Jennifer could do to keep from bursting into laughter, though she was shocked at Duffy's approach, as was the matron whose eyes seemed to be popping out of her head.

"You don't know where I been educated, pal. I graduated from Senn High School and then I went away to college."

"You went *away* to college?" Duffy said, pulling his note pad from his pocket and quickly leafing to the right page. "You call flunking out of the nursing program after four weeks at Harper Community College in Palatine because of reading deficiency *going away* to college?"

"I had to live with a girlfriend in the suburbs for a while."

"You apparently aren't going to answer my question."

"About Ed and Bobby? Sure, I'll answer it. They never hit me as bein' so bright. What's so special about writin' for a newspaper or bein' an almost jock in college? Why do they like me? I'm a fun girl– what can I tell ya?"

"You lied to me about Adrienne not knowing about you."

"Well, she knew about me. She knew me, you know? But she didn't know I was seein' Bobby."

"Were you aware that she had a key to his apartment?"

"I never thought about it much, but I don't guess it surprises me. They were engaged."

"You didn't worry about being caught in there with him?"

"There's a chain lock. Nobody's gettin' in there while we're in there unless we let 'em."

"Where were you going to go if Adrienne showed up?"

"I don't know. I never thought about it. Never happened." She chuckled. "Luckily."

"How did Bobby Block die?" Duffy asked.

"TV news says somebody poisoned him. Only I don't know what they put it in, 'cause like I say, he wasn't eatin', far as I could tell. Maybe they put it in his water."

"What were you doing in his apartment the night before?"

"What are you talkin' about?"

"You were there. Several witnesses saw you come and go."

"I'm not sayin' I wasn't there. I'm just wonderin' if you really don't know."

"In other words, it was just a social call."

"Right, exactly. Social. I mean, let's face it, Bobby and I were not an item. We didn't go out, you know what I mean? Adrienne got around, had a lot of friends. Anyway, I'm going with Ed, and just because he doesn't mind me seein' Bobby now and then, when I go out, I go out with Ed."

"Uh-huh, and you really think Adrienne didn't know about you and Bobby?"

"I don't think so."

"What were you doing at Adrienne's the day she died?"

"I was going to threaten her."

Now even Duffy was shocked.

"You were?"

"Yes, I was."

"Why?"

"Because I heard she was flirting with Ed."

"Adrienne was flirting with Ed?"

"That's right."

"And that's not good?"

She swore. "You're right."

"You can see Bobby on the side, even though he's engaged to Adrienne, but if Adrienne makes a move on your man, you're going to threaten her?"

"That's right."

"How does that compute?"

"How what?"

"How does that figure? Make that make sense for me-that it's OK for you to fool around with her guy, but it's not all right for her to make eyes at yours."

"I never said what I was doing was OK. But Ed didn't mind, and Adrienne didn't know, so I kept doin' it. If Ed didn't like it, he coulda tol' me. And if Adrienne found out, she shoulda put up a fuss, just like I was going to. If a woman don't fight for her man, she don't deserve to keep him."

"Uh-huh. So what were you going to do to Adrienne?"

"Just scare her a little. Hurt her if necessary."

"You're serious?"

"You heard me. I had a weapon. I'd have used it. I'd have killed her if she'd given me a reason."

"You amaze me, Josie."

"Yeah, why's that?"

"You're under arrest for murder, and I assume you want to talk your way out of it."

"Yeah."

"You're not doing a very good job."

"Well, I'm just tellin' the truth. I knew you had me at both places before Bobby and Adrienne were found, so I figured honesty was the best policy."

"That doesn't fit you."

"Honesty doesn't?"

"No."

"You heard me lie yet today?"

"You stretched it a little on going away to college."

"I did? I didn't mean to. Palatine may not seem far to you, buddy, but leavin' the city is a trip for me."

"So you went to Adrienne's to scare her and maybe even hurt her. What was your weapon?"

"A .22."

"Pistol?"

"Yeah."

"Ever use it before?"

"Nope."

"Would you have used it?"

"You bet."

"What would have made you use it?"

"If she gave me any grief."

"And did she?"

"Are you kidding? She answered my knock and dropped dead right there. I just shut the door and hit the bricks, man."

"How did you know she was dead?"

"I felt for a pulse at her neck. Nothing. Dead and I mean right away. Didn't that medical guy say Bobby was dead before he hit the floor too?" Duffy nodded. "Must have been the same way here. I thought about Bobby and knew the same person probably pulled both jobs. I didn't want any of it. But on the way out I saw a lot of people coming in, and I had to try to look like I hadn't just seen somebody drop dead right in front of me. Did a pretty good job hiding it too."

"Hiding it."

"The fact that I had just seen that. I think I looked pretty normal."

"Yeah, for someone driving a canary Porsche."

"Yeah, only it's yellow."

"Uh-huh."

Duffy stood and stretched. Josie lit another cigarette. "Something's still sticking in my craw," he said finally. She looked up. "It didn't bother you that this woman was still grieving the loss of her fiance?"

"Oh, sure, that's what made me feel so bad later. Ed finally told me I shoulda gone to him before running over to her place, because whoever told me that she was seeing Ed didn't know the whole story. I asked him what was the whole story, and he said she was just cryin' on his shoulder. I believe him now."

"Who told you about Adrienne seeing Ed?"

"A guy at the *Tribune*. Chris."

"Really? Does Ed know that?"

"No, and he ain't gonna know either. He likes Chris."

"Does Chris like him?"

"I know what you're driving at, but it's not true."

"You know for sure?"

"I sure do. It's something Chris likes people to think about him, but it's definitely not true. Thing is, I knew Chris long before I met Ed or Bobby."

"Wonderful."

"So what happens to me now? Can I go?"

"I'm afraid not."

"You don't believe me? You think I murdered these two people?"

"Actually I don't, but you were at both scenes. You had a motive in at least one case. I don't know if you studied enough nursing at Harper to figure out how to poison someone. But if I didn't detain you until we could clear you, I'd be delinquent in my duty."

"I was a juvenile delinquent once."

"You'd better get a lawyer, Josie."

"OK."

# Twelve

Cap Duffy roared when he heard the Chris Young parking lot story. Then he asked Jennifer what she thought of his interview with Josie Sisk.

"You were pretty tough with her, Cap. But I'll tell you this– I think she's innocent. I don't think she's got the brains to pull off a sophisticated poisoning."

"Unless she's dumb like a fox and a great actress. She was consistent anyway, wasn't she? I mean, we're talking about a girl with no light at the top of the stairs."

"Any more on the poison?"

"Yeah, I got a call from Jake just after I got back to the office this morning. First he gave me an evaluation of some of the medicines and stuff we found in Block's apartment. Mostly vitamins and minerals, but lots of 'em, which Block would have had to have taken if he was really on a starvation-type diet. And protein powder, just like the kind you can get from these home-based mail-order businesses.

"Jake said he sent some tissue sample to the Center for Disease Control in Atlanta. Their preliminary finding is that Block, at least, died of dioxin poisoning. They found one hundred parts per billion dioxin in his body fluid. One part per billion is considered hazardous to human health and has been known to cause cancer, liver damage, and birth defects.

"Jake says it's one of the most toxic substances known, and that with as dense a concentration as was found in Block's tissue, the man didn't have a chance."

"Could it have caused Block's cancer?"

"Oh, no, this would not have been in his system long before it killed him."

"How does that fit in with your theory– and Jake's– that it worked on a delayed release basis?"

"Good girl, Jenn. That's just the question the professional detective asked. Jake says they also found traces of some sort of a buffer, an agent that protects the system from the harmful effects of the poison for a brief period, not longer than twenty-four hours. And once that buffer has been eaten away or is absorbed into the system, the dioxin is left to its devices. Almost instantaneous death at that one hundred per billion concentration. They're sending a sample from Adrienne's body down there too."

"It'll show the same, won't it?"

"Likely."

"What do you make of their starvation diets? Were they setting themselves up for this? Is it still possibly a double suicide?"

"It's possible, but I can't figure the delayed effect part of it. If you're going to kill yourself, particularly in a double death pact, why not do it quickly and together? Who wants to inject himself and then wonder when it's going to happen?"

"Maybe he did it, and she knew how he did it, so she followed suit."

"Maybe," Duffy said. "But it isn't a normal double suicide modus operandi."

"It's not a normal *murder* modus operandi, Cap."

"True enough. That's another reason I doubt the suicide idea, even though I thought of it first. Where does a guy get access to dioxin? Jake says the only place he knows of is at one of the disease control centers, and you'd have to be a physician or a scientist to even study it. You'd have to be a criminal to remove it from the laboratory."

"Where do they get dioxin, Cap?"

"Researchers bring samples of contaminated floodwater in for analysis. When dioxin is found, people are evacuated from their homes, the substance becomes quarantined in the lab, and the local or state Department of Health moves in to treat the area."

Duffy agreed that Block's notebooks were the key to the success of the rest of the investigation, particularly when he got a glimpse of how detailed they were. "If Sisk is innocent, as I fear, we're probably looking for someone we haven't considered yet," he said.

"That's going to be the point of my first couple of columns about this case," Jennifer told him.

"Futility?"

"You bet. Dead ends. Long hours. Frustration. it's like running in a maze. You see an opening, you charge through, you hit a wall, you go back, you start over. You enjoy this?"

"I enjoy knowing that a break will come that will make everthing make sense. When it starts to fall into place, it'll all happen at once, and we'll be saying, "Ah ha! That's why this and that's why that.""

"I hope so."

"We have to stay optimistic, Jennifer. If you don't believe a break is coming, it's hard to stay in the game."

"Tell me one thing. Is this a typical investigation?"

"I'll say this: It's not a typical way to die, but it's a very typical investigation. It's like a crossword puzzle. If this word is right, these will be right; but if that word is wrong, we start from scratch. We're starting from scratch, in effect, now, but at least we've got a lot of the underbrush cleared away. We can start to get to the heart of the matter. We can say, who really did this if it wasn't all the people who could have or should have?"

"I think you just mixed a few metaphors there," Jennifer said, "but I see what you mean."

"Tell me what a metaphor is, and I'll try to unmix them for you."

"Forget it, Cap. That's my job. Listen, you're not sure about Sisk yet. How will you determine whether or not she's telling the truth?"

"About all I can do is assign some people to check out her background with a fine-tooth comb to see if there's a link to dioxin or someone with access to dioxin there anywhere. See, the poison that killed Block– and most likely Eden too– is the smoking pistol. Whoever's got the dioxin source has the means. None of the people we've investigated so far had more than motive and opportunity, and that's not enough. When the means is as bizarre as it is in this case, if we can find someone with the means, we may not have to work so hard to establish the motive and opportunity."

"Interesting," Jennifer said.

"Exhausting."

"I hear you."

Duffy paged carefully through the first Block notebook, which covered almost the first two weeks of January. "I can't make heads or tails of it," he admitted. "I can make out the dates and times, but little else. Can you read it, Jennifer?"

"I can read it, but it doesn't mean much to me either. See, here in mid-February of the fourth notebook I recognize his notes from a Police Department press conference we both attended."

"What's it say?" Duffy said. "Anything interesting?"

"Nah. It was just that thing about the police pension fund and benefit committee."

"Not interesting, all right. I had hoped these notebooks would reveal something good."

"You want me to just read through them aloud? You can make notes of anything you think is worth checking on."

"I guess."

For sounding so unenthusiastic about the exercise, Duffy took a ton of notes. Every time Jennifer read off a set of initials or tried to guess the meaning of an abbreviation, he jotted it down. Often he looked over her shoulder to help her make out a particularly scribbly entry. Their break came early that evening when she read a note entered 9:00 A.M., Monday, February 28.

It appeared like this:

Recd. perm. fr. PT on exp. Can use A if kp hm pstd.
Phd. BC off. for appt. Thu. 10.3 a K. Av.

Jennifer interpreted it this way, laboriously, for Cap:

"Received permission for, or maybe from— and I assume PT is someone's initials, yeah, the, uh, managing editor at the *Trib* is Phil Thornton. That a safe assumption then?"

"If you're sure that's his name— yeah, let's run with it."

"OK, then he received permission from Thornton on e-x-p. Hm. E-x-p."

"Explanation?" Duffy said.

"I don't think so. It's something he needs the boss's permission for."

"Experience?"

"Maybe. Permission for experience doing what? Something undercover maybe? Maybe it's an exposé on something or someone."

"E-x-p short for exposé?"

"Yeah!" Jennifer said. "I just said that, didn't I? OK, he received permission from Thornton for an exposé, but on what? Can use A if he keeps him posted. I don't know who A is, maybe someone else on the staff, but he can use A, I'm guessing, if he keeps Thornton posted. Why would he have to keep Thornton posted if he used someone else on staff? Maybe it's someone not on staff. Adrienne!"

"You're assuming a lot," Duffy said, "but keep going. He can use Adrienne in the exposé?"

"I think so. Then he phoned BC office. BC is obviously someone's initials. And got an appointment for Thursday at ten-thirty in the morning. K Avenue-oh boy, that could be anything."

Duffy furrowed his brow. "If I had the manpower, I'd call every place of business with the initials BC on every street in Chicago starting with a K and find out which one of 'em had an appointment with Block on— what would it be? Thursday, March third at ten-thirty in the morning."

"But Cap, you're assuming too much. We don't know if BC is a person's name or a company name. We don't know if the Thursday was the immediately following one. We don't know if Block used his own name in making the appointment, but I would highly doubt it. All BC would have to do, whoever that is, is see Bobby's name in the paper as a police reporter, and if the exposé is anything serious, Block is a dead man."

"I agree I don't have enough yet to start the search, Jennifer, but do you realize what you just said? You said if BC, the company or the person, found out who Block was, he'd be a dead man. And he is a dead man. You keep studying the notes– my advice would be to jump to the following Thursday– while I call, what was the editor's name?"

"Phil Thornton."

"Yeah, Thornton, to see if he knew any of the details."

Jennifer found the entry for Thursday, March 3 and read:

Init. int. unevent., BC not in. Set for diag. tsts., EKG, etc., Mon. No break. Mon. ur. samp.

At the bottom of the page, she read "Ken. Ave." and was eager to tell Duffy. He returned with bad news from Thornton.

"He really wants to help all he can, but he said he simply agreed in principle to Block's exposé– he makes it a practice not to involve himself, even to the point of not knowing the target. He just wants to know in advance in case legal questions arise. He was very curious to know where we got Block's notebooks. I told him we uncovered a lot of stuff in the course of the investigation."

Jennifer made a face at him.

"You didn't want me to tell him you stole them from Young who had stolen them from Block's desk, did you?" Duffy asked.

"No, but I didn't want to be responsible for your lying to him either."

"Did I lie to him?"

"By omission you did."

"Same way you did when you didn't tell me you were seeing Young in the park?" Duffy said. Jennifer winced. "You could have gotten yourself killed. He was a murder suspect, you know."

"I know. I almost killed *him* Cap."

She showed him the ently she had been studying. "If this is the address down here, that narrows it down some, it?" she said.

"Some. Kenmore? Kendale? Kendall? Kenwood? Should be able to find a BC on one of the Ken– something streets."

"But his use of BC this time makes it look more like a person, doesn't it? And if he has to bring a urine sample and have diagnostic tests the following Monday, is he meeting with a doctor? Is BC a doctor? It wouldn't be the same doctor who's treating his cancer if it's tied in with this exposé."

"If it is an exposé, Jennifer. We're still guessing."

"C'mon, Cap, we're onto something and you know it. Where's the optimism?"

"I left it in bed last night."

"Let's look at Monday the seventh of March."

Gluc. tst. Foul. Boring wtng. Fml. Orntl. Dr. elus. abt. educ., dbt. MD. BC not in. Off. grl. says seldm. Inj. appt. supp. Prt. Iks. Ik. commrcl. stf.

"Wow I'll admit you may be onto something, Jennifer. Translate that mess for me."

She studied it for several minutes. "I think he's saying he had a glucose test he didn't like, probably where they make you drink that concentrated Coke-type stuff. He waited a long time, like you do with those crazy tests, and he was bored. The next part I don't know. Is he saying there's a female doctor who's elusive about her education? He's doubting her M.D. degree?"

"What's 'Orntl.'?"

"I couldn't tell you, Cap. Ornithologist?"

"Ha!" he said. "Now I've got one on the brilliant columnist! He's going to a bird doctor?"

Jennifer smiled. "Chalk one up for Broderick Crawford. Twenty-one-fifty to headquarters."

"Headquarters by," he said. "Only a true 'Highway Patrol' devotee could appreciate that."

"You're talking to one," she said, extending her hand.

He shook it. "The originals?"

"Of course not," she said. "You've got me by ten years. Reruns only."

"I'm sure," he said, turning back to the notebooks. "I can see we're going to need Jake's input on this."

# Thirteen

Dr. Jacob Steinmetz arrived with a large brown paper bag filled with Chinese food carryout specialties. Trying to suppress a grin, he growled about having to work on a Saturday night, but it was apparent to Jennifer that he secretly enjoyed playing detective.

"Jennifer thinks she's onto something here, Jake," Duffy said, "and it's obvious to us we're heading in a medical direction."

Jennifer flipped back to the Monday, March 7, entry as they sampled Jake's gifts "I love Oriental food," she said.

"Oriental!" Cap said. "Maybe that's what 'Ornt,.' stands for!"

"Lemme see that," Jake said. "Wow, you guys are reaching. It could mean Oriental, I guess, but what does that tell you?"

Duffy took over. "That he had a foul, boring glucose test and that there was a female, Oriental doctor who was elusive when he asked about her education, so he doubted her medical degree."

Jake almost doubled over in laughter. "It sounds like a Peter Sellers movie! What else is there?"

Duffy was not amused. "If you see any other possibilities, Jake, we're open. We've been staring at this scribbling long enough."

With his mouth full, Jake waved an apology and bent over the notebook. Jennifer continued, "BC not in. I'm guessing now that that's the doctor he wants to see. Office girl says seldom?"

"That would fit," Jake agreed with a twinkle. "If he's the main doctor, he would seldom be in, right?"

"But what kind of a doctor is he?" Duffy said. "He gives glucose tests, EKGs, and all that."

"I don't know, Cap. There can be a lot of reasons for both those tests. What else can you make out here?"

"I haven't been able to make anything out of the next few lines," Jennifer admitted. "He's making some kind of a point here. What do you think?"

The three of them sat on the edges of their chairs and hunched were the little notebook, staring at the entry:

Inj. appt. supp. Prt. Iks.
lk. commrcl. stf.

Jake tried, "Injection appointment support. That makes no sense, and I don't know what p-r-t is."

"The capital P means a new sentence," Jennifer said, "so the first three words stand alone. I don't know what p-r-t is either, but the rest of that last line is 'looks like commercial,' um, maybe 'staff' or 'stuff'."

Steinmetz suddenly stood and bent from the waist, raising his glasses to his forehead and pushing his face a few inches from the page, blocking Duffys and Jennifer's view. "May I?" he said, picking up the notebook and carrying it near an overhead light.

"By all means," Duffy said, "What is it, Jake? What've you got?"

"If p-r-t means 'protein,' he's saying it looks like the commercial stuff, which is just what the lab thought of the stuff they found in his kitchen cupboards! BC could stand for bariatric clinic where they give these glucose tests and EKGs before starting people on these liquid protein diets!"

"Are they legit?" Jennifer asked. "Why would he expose them?"

"If they're prescribing stuff that they then supply, and it's commercial protein powder, then they're breaking the law. And of course, if the doctor's staffing his office with nonmedical personnel, they're likely counseling, diagnosing, and administering tests that only an M.D. is licensed to do."

Jake turned back to the page, then sat heavily as if it had all just hit him like a ton of bricks. "If i-n-j means injection, then a-p-p-t s-u-p-p could mean appetite suppressant, of which we found traces in both bodies! It *is* a bariatric clinic!"

"But why would he say BC is not in, if he was referring to a bariatric clinic?" Jennifer asked.

"Yeah," Duffy said, "and do you know of any bariatric clinics on a street like Kenmore, or Kendale, or Kendall, or Kenwood, or something like that?"

Steinmetz squinted in thought. "The only doctor I can think of on a K Street is Duke Creighton on Kendall. He's been known to follow the trends, put people on severe diets, that type of thing. Used to be quite the playboy too, owns a yacht and all the rest, but he's getting up there now. Must be close to retirement."

"Duke his real name?" Duffy asked, pulling a fat phone book off the top of a file cabinet.

"Seems maybe not," Jake said, "but I don't think I know his real name."

"Duffy leafed through the phone book, stopped in the Bs, ran his finger down the page and peered intently at the entry for Creighton on Kendall. He straightened up and twirled the book around on the table so it was right side up for Jennifer and Dr. Steinmetz.

They bent close to read: "Brewster (Duke) Creighton, general practice, specializing in nutrition and bariatrics."

"OK," Jake said, 'let's just slow down a minute. Block may have been doing some kind of a series on Creighton, and it may have been an expose. He may also have simply been on a doctor-supervised, liquid protein diet."

"Jake, it's the first solid lead we've got. Let me ask you something. Is there a traditional location for appetite suppressant shots?"

"Not really. It's fairly common to administer them to the patient just below the hip, while the patient is standing. But Cap, Duke Creighton is a fine physician. Always has been. Was some sort of a Chicago sports hero years ago, an Olympian or some such thing, maybe on a rowing team."

"So we shouldn't check him out because he rowed a boat for the U.S. of A., Jake?"

"I'm not saying that. I just think you have to move cautiously when you start accusing a renowned physician of running a clinic worthy of an exposé."

"That's not all I'd accuse him of, Jake," Duffy said. "I think he figured out who Block was and added a little something to Bobby's last appetite suppressant."

Jake looked stony, but he didn't argue.

"It'll all be in here if it's true," Jennifer said, patting the stack of notebooks.

The three spent until 11:00, P.M. piecing together startling information from the scribbled cryptic notes of a dead man.

On March 14 Bobby had involved Adrienne in the scam under the name Betty Miller.

The entry for March 17 revealed he was using the name Daniel Edmonds.

March 23 revealed a note that indicated that the office girl, a Kirsten Moon, had offered to aid him in getting more than he was entitled to from Blue Cross-Blue Shield for his treatments. "You pay $50, I put down that you paid $75, and they pay you 80 percent of that, or $60."

Block's notes indicated that he asked if she wanted a cut. "I wouldn't know what to do with more money," she had replied.

"It still doesn't prove anything about the murders," Jake said miserably, late in the evening. But his futile defense of an old acquaintance, one he admitted he had not seen for more than five years, was hollow and nearly unheard.

Block's research into the records of one of the leading home-based mail-order business in the country revealed that Dr. Brewster Creighton was its leading seller of protein powder and had won innumerable trips and other prizes.

"I can't believe Duke would do that," Jake lamented. "It's against the law to prescribe the stuff, and no doubt it's against the buying service rules too."

Jennifer interpreted a March 30 entry this way:

> My own doctor says the weight loss is OK and the protein and vitamins are not harmful, though the big C is acting up again. I'll look trim in the coffin.

"You gotta admit that's ironic," Duffy said, shaking his head.

"Big C mean colon or cancer?" Jennifer wondered.

"Either one," Jake said. "What's the difference?"

The April, 1 notes showed Block's confidence that his cover was still intact.

> I never want my picture in the paper like my former boss. Her undercover days are over.

April, 8, Block noted that he had told Phil Thornton that he would be ready with the first installment of the big exposé by the last week of April for the Sunday, May 1 *Tribune*.

> I asked if he wanted to know what it was all about. He said no, but if it was big enough he could try to get it in the *Tribune Magazine*. I said no, because once it broke, it would have to run everyday for at least a week. He asked if my weight loss had anything to do with it. I lied and said no. He'll find out soon enough.

April 19, Block wrote that he was looking forward to the appetite suppressant shot the next day.

> They start to wear off now after about five days. It's all I can do to hang on until Wednesday afternoons. Cheated only twice. No noticeable difference in weight loss pattern. Medical records

show no listing for Filipino female 'doctor' who handles most of
the work. Still have never seen BC. On his boat somewhere KM
says.

Several records indicated a discrepancy in charges and mode of
payment, depending on which of the staff waited on Block and/or
Adrienne. Her weight loss was slower and less dramatic, but she cheated
more.

The next entry, under the same date, made Jennifer teary.

Wrote to Jenn. Fence-mending long overdue. Guess I'll just tell
her straight out. No excuse, but a reason. Hope she agrees to see
me. Wouldn't blame her if not.

She only hoped he had gotten her message to phone back.

"I've got enough to get a warrant right now," Duffy said.

"You may be able to get a coroner on a Saturday night," Jake said. "But
I'd like to see you rouse a judge. Anyway, you don't know where to begin
to look for Creighton."

"I don't want Creighton yet. I just want access to his office tomorrow.
Nobody will be there on a Sunday. If I can get clearance for you, Jake,
will you join me? I'm gonna need help deciphering medical notes and
records."

"I guess so," Steinmetz said. "But this is going down hard."

"I can imagine, Duffy said. "How long have you known Creighton?"

"A couple of decades at least. I met him when we were both on an
emergency public safety board for the Fox Lake River flood project."

Jennifer and Duffy stared at him. He looked from one to the other before
realizing what he had said. Creighton was the type of doctor who would
have access to disease germ samples and poisons. Jake buried his head in
his hands.

"OK if I go now?" he asked finally.

"Sure, Jake. And thanks a lot. Can I call you tomorrow if I get the
warrant?"

Jake nodded.

"And you won't tell a soul what we uncovered here tonight until we
make an arrest, huh?"

He nodded again and pulled on his coat as he shuffled wearily out the
door.

"I'm sorry to be calling so late, Mrs. Cole. This is Detective Cap Duffy
of the Chicago Police Department calling for the Judge.... Thank you,
ma'am.

"Judge, I'm terribly sorry to wake you, and you know I wouldn't if it weren't important.... Yes sir, we met once in the late sixties during an Illinois Bureau of Investigation drug bust in the western suburbs when you were with the State's attorney's office, and we met again during the Tylenol murder investigations . . . in Mr. Fahner's office, yes sir.

"Well, it's this double poisoning murder of the newspaperman, Block, and his fiancee, Adrienne Eden.... Yes, sir, if I can get a warrant to search a doctor's office tomorrow, I feel confident we'll be able to make an arrest.... A messenger? No, sir, if you did that, I'd come myself to pick it up tonight.... Thank you, sir. I appreciate that. Here's the doctor's name and address."

The judge also recognized Creighton's name and asked several questions about the investigation before issuing a warrant that Duffy himself drove over to pick up.

When Duffy returned at about midnight, Jennifer had more information for him. "Look at this entry for April 15. It looks like he's saying, 'Told Mac about BC. Probably shouldn't have, but he'll keep it. A's appetite suppressant wore off early last week too. She had another yesterday morning.' So, Cap, Bobby has his next shot the following Wednesday afternoon and dies Thursday morning. She has hers that same Thursday morning, a week after this entry, and dies the next afternoon.

"You realize what that means, Cap? She had her injection and had that poison in her system by the time she showed up at his apartment just after noon on the day he died."

Cap still had his hat on, and now he pushed it back on his head and folded his arms. "What we have to determine tomorrow is how Creighton got onto Block and Eden and who gave the lethal injections. If one of these office girls did it, which is unlikely, whether Creighton himself actually prepared the shots, or whether he even administered them. Anything on that in Block's notebook?"

"No. The twelfth book ends April sixteenth. He died on the twenty-first."

"Well, there should be a lot of corroboration in the doctor's office, unless he was smarter or more careful than we thought. I'm gonna grab some shut-eye and then visit that office first thing in the morning. You?"

"I'm afraid I can't join you tomorrow, Cap."

"What? We're getting to the best part, lady!"

"I know, but I go to church on Sundays, and I try to work as little as possible."

He smiled at her. "Where do you go to church?"

"These days up in Waukegan at Jim's church."

"How about a deal?"

"A deal?"

"Yeah. My wife and I will join you for church, then you two join Jake and me at the doctor's office."

"Jim would love that."

"Yeah. My wife doesn't like that snooping around sort of stuff, so I'd drop her off at home maybe after dinner and before we head to Creighton's office."

"You're not worried about losing time on this?"

"Nah. The only other people who know about it are Jake and the judge, and they won't be telling anyone. I'll be hard pressed to get any help rounding up Creighton on a Sunday anyway. My plan is to get everything we need at his office and try to collar him Monday. We got a deal?"

"Sure, Cap. Are you sure you want to?"

"If your church is like the one I went to when I was nine, where they still believe, how did you say it– ?"

"That there's a God who loves you and a Jesus who saved you from your sins?"

"Yeah. Then I'd like to check it out. It'll be a little late notice for Maryann, but she's always game."

# Fourteen

Cap and Maryann Duffy were so impressed with Jim's church that they asked if they could come back the following week.

"You could even come tonight," Jim said at lunch.

"That would be even better," Maryann said, surprising everyone, including herself. "I mean, it's just that everyone seemed so happy and at ease and-well, enthusiastic."

"We are," Jennifer said.

"What impressed me," Cap said, "was how obvious it was that everyone just believes. I mean, they talk about it, sing about it, pray about it, smile about it."

"Not it," Jim said, smiling.

"Yeah," Cap said, slightly embarrassed. "I know." He pointed up.

"I was almost going to join you on your little escapade this afternoon," Maryann said, "just so maybe we could talk a little more about it. But if we're going tonight, I won't have to."

"I don't know how you can pass it up," Jennifer said.

"Believe me, it's easy," she said. "I know it's important, and I'm proud that Harold is good at it. But it always gives me the willies to be poking around in other people's things."

"But we have a warrant, Hon," Cap said.

"I know, and if that makes you comfortable, enjoy yourselves. I"ll pass."

"But you will come tonight?" Jennifer asked.

"I wouldn't miss it," she said. "I confess it was not at all what I expected. I was really afraid at first and almost didn't come. But Harold told me about the good times he'd had in church as a child, so I thought it was worth a try. It left me with a million questions, I'll tell you that."

"Well," Jim said, "we don't have all the answers, but you can try us, and we can at least point you to someone who could be more helpful."

Dr. Jacob Steinmetz was waiting in his car across the street from Brewster Creighton's office when Cap Duffy pulled up with Jim and Jennifer.

Cap stopped next to Jake's car, and it was immediately obvious that the coroner was in a bad mood. "Let's park a couple of blocks down and not appear so obvious," Cap suggested. "I've tipped off the burglar alarm company and the local precinct station in case we can't get past the wiring, but Jim has the tools we need."

"Duke is in town," Jake said.

"How do you know that?" Cap asked.

"I couldn't help myself, Cap. I drove past his place. His mobile home is parked at the side, and the boat's in the garage. I saw him in the yard this morning."

It was all Duffy could do to keep from exploding. "Did he see you, Jake? If you blew this thing for us, he could have already been in there destroying all the evidence and— "

"I didn't say anything to him, Cap. He didn't see me. But I almost wish I had tipped him off."

"What if he's guilty?" Cap asked.

"That's the only thing that kept me from it. That, and the fact that you made me promise last night. I'm a man of my word, Cap. But breaking into a doctor's office goes against everything I've ever believed in."

"So does murder, doesn't it, Doctor?"

Jake stared at him. Cap pointed down the street, and Jake followed him. When the cars were situated, Jake joined the other three in Cap's car. "Jim will go first," Cap said, "and try to get in without tripping the alarm. Once he's in, we follow nonchalantly, as if the office is open and we're expected."

"You don't see any value at all in allowing Duke to come down here and let you in so you don't have to break into his files and everything?" Jake tried.

"Doc, I gotta tell ya, that's a little naive. He'll call a lawyer to get a temporary restraining order on the warrant, and that will give him all the time he needs to destroy anything that would prove his guilt."

"Or innocence," Jake said.

"If there's nothing in the office that implicates him, then maybe he is innocent. We're not gonna plant anything, Jake. I'm going in there with you and one of the straightest cops I've ever worked with. Jim is Officer Friendly, for pete's sake, and Jennifer would never let me get away with anything underhanded, which I wouldn't try anyway. You can be of great help to me today, Jake, if you're not just in there trying to defend your buddy."

"He's not my buddy," Jake said, "but he's a brother in the profession."

"He also took the Hippocratic oath, right?" Cap said.

Jake nodded.

"And if he violated that, you want to see him answer for it just as much as I do, maybe more."

Cap took Jake's lack of response as consent and nodded to Jim, who left the car and walked briskly a block and a half to the Creighton Medical Building. Jim tried the front door, then moved around to the back where he slipped a thin strip of metal between the door and its frame, slicing the wire to the burglar alarm. That took care of the remote feed to the police station, but opening the door would trip the local siren on the building.

Jim used a bent wire pick to trip the lock almost as quickly as a key would have done the job, then placed one hand on the glass next to the door and the other hand on the handle. He spotted the wire to the siren inside the building. He yanked open the door and heard the scream of the horn as he raced through the shallow lobby and swiped at the nearly hidden wire with his metal strip. The siren ceased.

Jim returned and relocked the back door, then made his way through to the front where he unlocked the door and pushed it open a few inches to signal the others to join him. When they were in, Jim locked the front door and moved cautiously toward Creighton's private office. He dropped to the floor and peered through the crack under the bottom of the closed door.

He motioned to Cap to join him in the front lobby again. "There's a unit next to Creighton's desk that could be any medical device, but if it is, it's the only one in that office."

"What are you saying? What do you think it is?"

"A sound-activated alarm."

"Have no fear," Duffy said with a grin, and he produced from his pocket a high frequency tone generator.

"You think of everything, don't you?" Jim asked.

"I'm an old thirty-nine," Cap said. "There's a reason for that. Would you like to do the honors?"

"Sure, what do I do?"

"Just aim it at the machine and give it one shot with this button. You won't hear a thing, but if we were outside, dogs would come running."

Purcell edged back to the door and carefully laid the corner of the palm-sized device in the crack under the door. He pushed the button. "How do I know if it worked?" he whispered.

Like this," Cap said, and he rapped loudly on the door. "Gimme your pick." And he popped the lock. The device had indeed been a sound detector, and if it had been on, it was now off.

"Did I do that?" Purcell asked.

"We'll never know," Cap said. "But who cares? We now own this place."

After a quick tour to get the lay of the land, Duffy pulled everyone back into Creighton's private office. "It's possible that people in the neighborhood are already suspicious. If they call the cops, a squad will come and then tell them that we're authorized to be here. If they call Creighton, we could have trouble when he shows up. If anyone notices him arrive, let me know so I can get some back up. Since he's unaware of this, he could shoot us and not suffer for it.

"Jennifer, I want you to dig through the files in the reception area. See what you can find on Bobby and Adrienne's aliases, Daniel Edmonds and Betty Miller. Jake, check the medicine storage cabinets. You know what you're looking for."

"Dioxin," he said.

Duffy nodded. "I'll go through the doctor's office, and Jim will float around, opening anything you want opened, damaging as few locks as possible. Jake?"

"Yeah."

"If you find anything significant, don't touch it, hear?"

Jake nodded.

"Work quickly, because if someone does tip off Creighton, he'd be here how fast, Jake?"

"Oh, forty minutes I guess."

"All right, we meet back here in twenty-five minutes with whatever you've got."

Jake found six vials of unidentified substances that were clearly labeled as dangerous poisons. Yet they were in the same cabinet as the appetite suppressant. He wondered whether the poisonings could have been a mistake and if other victims might turn up. Yet the poisons would have to be evaluated to see if they contained dioxin.

Jennifer found a raft of information on patients Edmonds and Miller from appointment times to payment receipts, from prescriptions to diagnostic test results. She found one report that seemingly indicated a cancer-related blood problem, along with a note that the information was classified and not to be discussed with the patient. Attached to this report was a handwritten note from Dr. Creighton stating that this 'problem shall in no way affect or be affected by the protein diet program."

But she also found strange financial documents. The K. M., who must have been Kirsten Moon, had indeed falsified many records to Blue Cross Blue Shield, initiating overpayments to patients from that company.

The plum of Jennifer's search was a small stack of notes concerning Edmonds and Miller that began early in March. The first several were copies of notes to Dr. Creighton that Mr. Edmonds was continually requesting an appointment with him. The doctor's replies recommended stalling as long as possible, promising that perhaps he would see Edmonds in May, if his schedule cleared.

Suddenly, on April 18 there was a note from another girl in the office to Miss Moon, informing her that the doctor had called from his Wisconsin cabin on the weekend to find out when certain patients were scheduled for appointments. The note added, "Kirstie, please call Dr. C. at his cabin and tell him when the following six are scheduled." Among the list were both Edmonds and Miller.

A general note went to the staff the afternoon of April 18, informing them that the doctor would be in Wednesday afternoon and Thursday morning and could then be reached at his home until Sunday afternoon at three when he would return to Wisconsin.

Duffy had all but struck out until he searched the cabinets lining the walls of Creighton's office. He had been through correspondence files, a petty cash fund, prescription pads, and equipment chests. But in one corner of a locked door of a locked cabinet was a small cash box, also locked. When Jim popped it open for him, Duffy knew he'd hit pay dirt.

In the box he found just over $11,000 in cash and a small ledger book with a rubber band around it, noting various payments and deposits. Creighton had apparently kept a stash of $20,000 in the box. But a payment was noted for Thursday evening, April 21, for $8,950 "to retire E.M. auto loan."

Duffy made a fast phone call to an associate and asked him to check telephone and bank records on two people, one of whom was Dr. Brewster Creighton. When Jennifer told Cap what she'd found, Duffy asked his boss to stake out the streets around the Creighton residence to see if he indeed planned to leave at 3:00 P.M. It was two-thirty.

When everyone had gathered in Creighton's office, Duffy summarized. "We can place Creighton himself here at the time of Block's and Eden's last injections. Whether he administered them or not, we don't know. He could have prepared them anyway, then this Kirsten Moon or someone else could have given the shots without being aware of the contents of the syringes.

"We'll have to examine the vials," Jake reminded him.

"Of course. The key is, what made Creighton call from Wisconsin last weekend and decide to come in when Block and Eden were scheduled for appointments? Obviously, someone tipped him off, but who was it and how did they get his number in Wisconsin?"

"Would it had to have been either Young, McDevitt, or Sisk?" Jennifer asked.

"Likely," Duffy said. "Sisk probably knew nothing about it. What motive would she have had for exposing the scam? Young may have had the notebooks before Block died, but I can't figure his motive either. He told you, Jennifer, that he hadn't read them, but for some reason he thought they might be important. Does that add up?"

"Really it does," Jennifer said. "As a newspaperman, he would know that there would be detailed information in there, even if he didn't read it."

"When was that entry in Block's journal that said he had told someone about BC?"

Jennifer pulled out the notebooks. "Friday, April fifteenth. Says he told Mac. What are you thinking, Cap? McDevitt?"

"Could be. Say McDevitt calls here to rat on Block because he can't stand sharing Josie with him. He wants to sell the doctor some information that would save his practice from a ruinous exposé. The doctor isn't in, and to protect him, the staff probably says they can't give out his number but that they will call the doctor and give him a message. McDevitt makes the message provocative enough that Creighton indeed calls him back. Within a day or two, Creighton makes arrangements to be back in his office for the two appointments, and once the deeds are done, he settles with McDevitt."

"But what do you make of the cash journal entry, Cap?" Purcell asked.

"A good way to launder the money," Duffy said. "It goes from Creighton to McDevitt in cash, McDevitt deposits it in his account, then writes a check for that amount to pay off his car loan. He's that much richer because he now has the money he would have spent over the next three or four years in high car payrnents, but he's not all of a sudden flashing bills around. I've got someone checking on his bank statement right now. They'te also working on the phone calls between here and Creighton's Wisconsin cabin during the last week."

The phone rang, and everyone looked to Duffy. "All right," he said, "it could be my man, or it could be that someone has tipped off Creighton. Jennifer, you answer it, and if it's Creighton, make him think it's his answering service."

She picked up the phone. "Doctor's office."

"Dr. Duffy, please."

She smiled and handed Duffy the phone. "Yeah, Frank.... Oh, no! No mistake? Thanks, and stay close. We may need you. I may have to bluff him pretty good, but we"ll want to make the arrest today."

Duffy hung up without another word and began scrambling to put the office back in shape. "My guys are tailing Creighton. He and his wife have left the house in their mobile home, but it appears they're headed this way.

Jake, you and Jennifer and I will make it look like we haven't been here while Jim finds us a place inside here to wait for him."

# Fifteen

It seemed to take longer to put the office back the way it was than it had to put it in disarray. And things were slowed when Jim returned by Duffy's deciding to let him reorganize Creighton's office while Cap was on the phone to his contacts, pushing for information before Creighton showed up.

Jim had located a second floor hallway that overlooked the back lobby and much of the reception area where at least three of them could watch Dr. Creighton as he entered. Duffy, because of his size, would fit in a cabinet at one end of Creighton's office, and, blocked by a file cabinet, he could leave the door open far enough to view most of the room.

Meanwhile, with Duffy on the phone, Jim straightening Creighton's office, Jennifer tidying up the reception area, and Jake on the lookout after having relocked the medicine cabinets, they awaited Brewster Creighton.

"I see a couple of cars near yours!" Jake said. Duffy quickly ended his call and jogged to the front door. He peered down the street through the tinted glass lobby and pulled a walkie-talkie from his belt.

"One-nineteen to one-sixteen."

"One-sixteen," came the static filled response.

"Bill, you don't want three unmarked squads that close together and that close to this building, do you?"

"Ten-four, Cap. Repositioning. Any guess where the mark will pull in?"

"Ten-four, sixteen. Vehicle size should force him into north parking lot entrance. He's likely to enter the building from the back. What do we know about his current ten-twenty?"

"Stand by."

In less than a minute, Duffy's associate came back on with Creighton's approximate location and said, "E.T fifteen-hundred-fifteen."

"What's he saying?" Jake asked.

"Estimated time of arrival is three-fifteen," Cap said. "Everybody ready?"

"What'd you get on the phone and bank stuff, Cap?" Jim asked.

"Plenty."

Dr. Steinmetz, Jim, and Jennifer stationed themselves on the second floor, overlooking the back door, the main hallway, and the reception area, while Duffy climbed into the cabinet in Creighton's office.

"Nineteen to sixteen."

"Go ahead, Cap."

"Let me know when you spot the vehicle. I'll go off the air but will click you twice if I need you."

"How do we get in, sixteen?"

"Stand by," Duffy said, then hollered, "Jim?"

"Yeah!"

"You'd better unlock the front door— in case we need help."

"What if he comes to the front door? If it's unlocked it'll tip him off."

"He may already know we're in here, Jim. That may be why he's coming. Well, pick a door to leave unlocked so I can tell my backups."

"I'll unlock the back, Cap."

Duffy told his backup.

At seventeen minutes after three, Duffy's walkie-talkie crackled the message. "Nineteen to sixteen, vehicle sighted. Entering north lot. Parking at edge of lot in back. Driver leaving vehicle. Heading toward back door."

"I'm going off the air, sixteen!" Cap said, "And we're switching your unlocked door." Then he yelled, "Jim! Lock the back door fast and unlock the front. Hide where you can. This is it!"

Jim could see Brewster Creighton across the back parking lot about thirty feet from the back door, walking slowly, head down. Jim put one foot on the railing and leaped to the first floor, bending low as he hit to cushion the impact. He flew into the lobby and turned the knob on the back door, stealing a glance at Creighton before running back through the hallway. The doctor did not appear to have seen him.

Jim slid into the front lobby and unlocked the door, but as he turned to dash back upstairs, he heard Creighton inserting his key into the burglar alarm shutoff, then into the back door. Jim plastered himself against the wall in the lobby and held his breath.

Creighton moved purposefully through the main hallway carrying a black leather duffel bag. The broad, only slightly hefty, grey-haired doctor wore white buck shoes, rustcolored trousers, a white turtleneck sweater, and a pale yellow sports coat. He opened examining room doors on either side of the hall, quickly scanned them, and shut the doors again. Occasionally he would drop something in his bag.

When he got to the reception area, he pulled two of his medical degree certificates from the wall, then rummaged in the bottom of the desk drawer and replaced them with old photographs. At the end of the hall, he took down a photo of himself and the rest of the 1940 United States Olympic rowing team and replaced it with a photocopy of his undergraduate diploma.

He also retrieved a couple of photographs of his wife and family, one of his parents, and a gold inlaid letter opener. From a hallway closet he took his golf clubs and shoes and a camel hair sports coat. He then made a quick trip to his motor home, chatted briefly with his wife as he dropped off the stuff, and returned to the building.

He surveyed the rest of the first floor one more time, picking up a few keepsakes here and there and dropping them into his coat pockets. From one of the medicine cabinets he removed the six vials Jake Steinmetz had identified as poisonous. Just outside his office he inserted a special key into a mechanism above his door to turn off the soundactivated alarm, then unlocked his door. Inside he moved quickly to a cabinet at the other end of the office from where Duffy hid.

Dr. Creighton slid open a door and pulled an expensive leather briefcase from the shelf and placed it carefully on his desk. He opened it and emptied nearly $80 from his petty cash fund into it, replacing the box in his desk drawer. He pulled two folders from his file cabinet-stepping within three feet of the motionless Detective Cap Duffy paused only briefly to leaf through them, and deposited them in his briefcase as well.

Creighton looked around the room once more and retrieved a couple of personal knickknacks and keepsakes, packing them neatly in his case. He then unlocked the cabinet in the corner, unlocked the smaller door, unlocked the cash box, and left it open.

Creighton went to the phone, dialed a number he read from a tiny slip of paper, let it ring once, then hung up. He closed his briefcase, spun the combination locks, unplugged the sound alarm, and sat on the edge of the desk, looking at his watch.

Within seconds the phone rang once and fell silent. As if on cue, Creighton slid the briefcase off the desk, left his office without relocking the door, left the building without resetting the central alarm, and locked the back door. He strode to his vehicle and pulled away.

"He's gone!" Jim shouted from the front lobby.

"He get anything significant?" Duffy asked, turning on his radio and announcing that he was back on the air.

"He took the poison," Jake called as they met in the hallway.

Duffy called his backup. "Nineteen to sixteen. Bill, he set this place up for someone. Don't let him get too far. He's got evidence we need, and we can't let him dump it. Let him get out of sight of here and take him."

"Is he armed, nineteen?"

"I doubt it, but be careful." He turned to the others. "Let's clear out so we can stake this place out. Someone is coming, probably after dark. Anyway, I need time to figure out why Creighton takes eighty bucks and leaves more than $11,000 unlocked."

By early evening Maryann Duffy had been called to cancel her evening plans with her husband and Jim and Jennifer. Jake Steinmetz had received permission to go home. Jim had been stationed with one of the three back-up cars situated within view of the front of the building.

Jennifer was in the backseat of Duffy's squad car, now positioned on an east-west street a half block behind the medical building, with a clear view of the parking lot and back door. Duffy sat behind the wheel, alternately watching and reading a report hastily scribbled by one of his men, telling of the telephone bank activity of Brewster Creighton. Several of Creighton's phone calls from Wisconsin and his office had been to a pay phone on the Northwestern campus.

Duffy had also been filled in on the preliminary questioning of Dr. Brewster Creighton, who had refused to answer any questions until his lawyer arrived. The vials had been sent to the lab, and the results, showing concentrated dioxin content, came back at about the time Creighton's lawyer arrived.

Creighton apparently refused to tell even his lawyer what he had done in his office, other than pick up a few items. The lawyer had demanded that charges be filed or his client released, but the Homicide Division was stalling as long as possible, using Sunday as an excuse not to have all the documents and personnel they needed and knowing they'd have an easier time if they had Creighton's accomplice.

At approximately 11:30 P.M., after Jennifer had exhausted her "what-if" questions and was beginning to wonder if they weren't on a wild goose chase– which, Duffy told her, was not only entirely possible, but probable, given the odds in such situations– Duffy was informed by radio that an old car had been parked about three and half blocks from his location and that the driver was now walking in that direction.

Duffy and Jennifer peered out and soon saw a figure approaching from the north, occasionally illuminating a piece of paper in its hand with a penlight. Reaching the north edge of the parking lot to the medical building, the figure stayed in the shadows near a row of hedges and then angled directly toward the back door.

Duffy left his car with Jennifer right behind him and sidled up to the hedge row to watch the figure unlock the back door, apparently with a key. As the figure edged down the hallway, again illuminating the paper with a light, Duffy crept through the back door and deftly stayed about thirty feet behind, Jennifer still on his heels, her heart racing.

The figure located Creighton's office door and pushed it open, using the light constantly now. Duffy and Jennifer slipped off their shoes and stole down the carpeted hallway, stopping a few feet from the office.

From inside, they could hear the opening of the cabinet, the inner door, the box. Money was being stuffed in pockets. Duffy sneaked to the other side of the door where he could see in through the crack.

The figure reached inside a short coat and withdrew two thin pint bottles, which looked like whiskey containers. These were splashed around the floor from the cabinet, past the desk, and to the door, where the figure now stood not four feet from where Duffy crouched, his hand on the snubnosed .38 in his shoulder holster.

As the odor of gasoline wafted into the hallway, the dark figure pocketed the penlight and produced a disposable cigarette lighter. Backing up and reaching for the door behind it, the intruder carefully held it open, still gazing into the office, lighter poised.

Duffy moved up from behind and stuck the barrel of his pistol into the back of the man's neck, just above the spine, reaching around to the chin with his left hand. "Drop it or you're a dead man, Ed," he said, as McDevitt jumped, then struggled. The tall collegian whimpered and pulled against the force of Duffy's strangle hold, and somehow ignited the lighter and flipped it into the room.

The force of the blast drove both men into the hallway, and Duffy's gun bounced near McDevitt. Ed grabbed it and handed it to the detective, swearing and screaming. "Kill me, you liar! You said I'd be a dead man! Shoot me! Shoot me!"

Duffy holstered his weapon as flames from the office licked at the hallway. McDevitt lay in a heap on the floor, sobbing. "I had to make Bobby pay!" he said. "I had to make him pay!"

"You're *all* going to pay," Duffy said, grabbing the big man by his collar and his belt and using his own little strength and balance to drag McDevitt toward the back. Jennifer held the door open as Duffy yanked McDevitt to his feet and sent him stumbling past the bushes and safely out of range of the roaring fire.

Backup cars slid into the lot, and Cap's aide from the Chicago Avenue station jumped out and ran toward the back door, shouting for Duffy.

"Over here, Bill!" Cap called. 'We're all OK."

As Ed McDevitt was handcuffed and led to a squad car, Cap squeezed Jennifer's shoulder. She was shaking. He winked at her. "You and Jim up to a little coffee at my place later tonight? We owe it to Maryann, don't we?"

Jennifer could hardly speak. "Ask him," she said, as Jim came charging around the corner of the burning building. He threw his arms around her and held her tight, not thinking, or at least not caring, that it was the first time he had held her in front of anyone.

Relief lit his face as it sank in that Jennifer was safe.

Samatha Stanton is thrilled with life. She manages a thriving travel agency, and her marriage is good. That's why Jennifer is skeptical when Samantha's death is ruled a suicide. Then Jennifer starts to dig. What is going on with the travel agency business, and what is all the mystery about the self-euthanasia meetings? The police may think Samantha's death was a suicide, but Jennifer is going to find out what really happened.

Jerry B. Jenkins, is the author of more than fifty books, including the popular Margo Mystery Series, co-author of the best-selling *OUT OF THE BLUE* with Orel Hershiser, and *HEDGES*. Jenkins lives with his wife Dianna, and three sons at Three-Son Acres, Zion, Illinois.

# Jerry B. Jenkins

# GATEWAY

## Book Four In The Jennifer Grey Mystery Series

Flip over for another great
Jennifer Grey Mystery!
**TO LATE TO TELL**

**BARBOUR BOOKS**
Westwood, New Jersey

# GATEWAY

# One

Jennifer Grey and her fiance, Jim Purcell, sat silently in the west parlor of the Norman Funeral Home on Chicago's Near North Side.

None but the macabre enjoy funeral homes. But those who have lost close loved ones develop a particular aversion to them. It can resurface and drag them back to wrenching memories at the mere smell of a sickeningly sweet floral shop years later.

Jennifer herself had been widowed young. So quickly, so painfully, that it had taken her months to regain a semblance of normalcy in her life. She had not been married a year when her husband was killed on the highway.

But she had dealt with that. Time, so the cliché goes, was a healer. So were close parents; understanding friends; a good church. And when she carefully ventured out into the real world again, Jennifer found she could function alone.

The loss made her reluctant to untie her emotions, hesitant to respond to her cautious new admirer. For a while she was able to hide, even from herself, her deepest feelings for Jim. Only sharing their own crisis and learning to depend upon each other had brought her to where she could no longer pretend she didn't care for him.

And now, after a long courtship, they would be married in a few months. She had said yes to Jim, resulting in the second to the last change in her life since her first husband's death. Until now, most of the changes had been for the better.

She had moved from the women's page of the *Chicago Day* to the newsroom under legendary City Editor Leo Stanton. She and Jim had survived an ordeal in his career on the police force that, while it seemed to Jennifer almost as grieving as losing a mate, was really the beginning of their love relationship. She had been promoted to columnist with her own location on the front page.

Jim had only recently been promoted to sergeant and would soon be a plainclothes detective. Today he sat stiffly in his dress blues, wearing his funeral face, the one worn by all who were only loosely associated with the deceased.

Even Leo had been promoted. He had become managing editor just two months before. That meant a huge office on the sixth floor, a secretary, more business suits, less action, more headaches. He pretended not to like it, to be hemmed in, restricted from the fun of the daily grind, the hands-on editing.

But in truth Leo loved it. He deserved it. He had more policy input on the entire paper. Jennifer missed the measured casualness of dress that had characterized his reign of mock terror in the city room.

Leo had always been one for soft leather loafers or wing tips, gray woolen slacks, pastel button-down shirts, navy or camel blazers, always draped neatly over a chair by mid-morning.

He liked to loosen his tie and roll up his sleeves, but there was still something formal about that informality. Worst, he had always felt the need to temper the whole Ivy league look with a soggy, unlit cigar lodged in his right cheek.

He never smoked and frequently reminded everyone of that. Somehow, during the several weeks since he'd been promoted, he'd given up the cigar. Everyone guessed that Publisher Max Cooper had made it a prerequisite.

Jennifer nodded red-eyed at her many colleagues as they somberly stepped into the chapel. Mr. Cooper and his stately, white-haired wife sat near the front, behind the family. How strange not to hear his loud voice, his bellowing laughter. He had a reputation for bluster behind closed doors, but with the rank and file, he always seemed to feel required to joke and laugh and tell inane stories.

Jennifer turned to glance at Jim. His uniform made him look so young. The hat in his lap had left its telltale impression on his whitish-blond hair. His pale blue eyes noticed her looking up at him, and he pressed his lips together to acknowledge her.

The parlor was nearly full, though there was a line back to the lobby where many were still signing the guest book. Jennifer leaned to one side and peered up to the front row where the family sat, still stunned at their loss of just three days.

Leo sat in the middle of a nine-chair row, his left arm around his married daughter who sat next to her husband and their two young children. They had flown in the morning before from California. Leo's right arm was around his bachelor son from Maryland, who sat next to his mother's best friend—June Roloff—and her husband, Kent, assistant managing editor at the *Day*.

Someone had coached the grandchildren, who only occasionally looked at each other to whisper. Jennifer watched Leo for several minutes and wondered if he had even blinked. She didn't see him move.

He just stared straight ahead, not tightening his embrace on either his son or daughter, not looking at them, not speaking to them. It didn't appear he was crying. He simply sat with his arms around his family, like a statue.

Directly in front of him and about ten feet beyond lay the body of Samantha, his handsome, red-haired wife of thirty-seven years.

One of Jennifer's hands hid her eyes as she lowered her head and cried for Leo. Jim held her other hand in both of his. She had not known what to say to Leo from the moment she had heard of Samantha's death. She knew what not to say, and from her too-fresh memories of just a few years before, she decided her silent presence was the best she had to offer.

Had it been over a month ago that she and Jim had visited the Stantons' home? Jennifer had been amazed at the beauty and charm of their old West Town neighborhood place, a narrow, three-story Georgian brick they had lived in since their marriage.

Jennifer had met Leo's wife at office functions, of course, but she had never been to their home until Samantha called one morning and asked if she and Jim wanted to celebrate their engagement over dinner.

Jennifer laughed at herself for being surprised that Leo would even share such news with his wife. He didn't seem the type, but then, certainly, it was the type of thing a man would talk about with his wife.

Samantha had been in her usual bubbly form the morning she phoned. Her unusually low voice and rumbling chortle were in fine fettle as she joked about planning such an evening without Leo's knowledge.

"You wouldn't really, would you?" Jennifer had asked, alarmed, making Samantha guffaw all the more.

"'Course not, Honey. But it'd be fun, wouldn't it, to see the look on that ol' bulldog's face when company shows up for dinner? Ha! The biggest surprise for him would be something decent to eat, know what I mean?"

Jennifer liked the woman immediately.

Their home was quaint and lovely, as one might expect when the wife is a world traveler and the man runs in fast company. Samantha was co-owner of a travel agency and taught a night school college course in oil painting.

At first Jim and Leo seemed a bit ill at ease with each other that night. Neither was a big sports fan, but each felt obligated to talk about the Bears and the Blackhawks, under the assumption that the other wanted to.

When the ice was finally broken and they admitted that their real love was literature, they headed to Leo's study to discuss the editor's library. As they moseyed down the hall toward the book-lined cherrywood paneled

den, Jennifer heard Leo tease, "So how does a literate, nonjock wind up a cop, anyway?"

"He scream and holler at you a little now and then?" Samantha asked Jennifer after dinner.

"I was going to ask you the same thing," Jennifer said, laughing.

"No, he doesn't," Samantha had said, suddenly serious.

"I didn't think so."

"Then why were you going to ask?"

"Because he screams and hollers a lot at the office. Yet here he seems so peaceful. And I like the way he's not afraid to hold your hand or put his arm around you in front of people. It's almost out of character for him."

"I know what you mean, Jennifer. After all these years, too. I love it."

"You're lucky."

"Don't I know it," Samantha said. And with a twinkle she added, "And so is he."

"Don't you two ever fight?"

"Nope. I do, but he doesn't. I'm the one with the Irish temper."

"And he isn't?" Jennifer couldn't hide her incredulity.

Samantha smiled and tucked her feet up under her on the sofa. "That's what so many of his employees say," she said. "You should have seen him with our kids."

"Tough?"

"The opposite. A pussycat."

Jennifer shook her head slowly.

"All his employees do that," Samantha said. "Nobody believes me."

"Because you're putting us on, or because he's so consistently on our cases at the office?"

"Well, I'm not putting you on," she said. "I think jumping all over his employees is just his way of drawing the best out of people. He drew the best from you, didn't he? You were on the society page or the women's page or something, weren't you? Now you're better known than he is."

"Which is a little embarrassing for me," Jennifer admitted.

"And which suits him just fine," Samantha said.


The following week in the office, Jennifer had chatted with Leo about Samantha. "You don't talk about her that much," she said.

"Sam? Nah, I guess not. Think about her all the time, though."

"I wouldn't have believed that until I saw how you treated her the other night."

"We get along."

"You do better than get along. You enjoy each other."

"Yeah, and after all these years."

"That's what she said, Leo. Has it always been that good?"

"Mostly. Never any big problems. We disagree on politics, you know."

"Really? She's not a conservative?"

"Anything but. Kids are the same. Drives me nuts. We don't talk about it much."

"You have a super marriage," Jennifer said.

"You sound surprised."

"No, it's just that good marriages are so rare these days."

"I know they are, but that's not why you're surprised. You think the only good marriages belong to you religious types."

"Leo, you know religion has nothing to do with—"

"Yeah, yeah, all right. Born againers, then. Christians, evangelicals, whatever. You think they're the only ones with good anything. Good relationships. Good morals. Good marriages."

"Not necessarily. They have bad relationships too."

"Yeah, but they're the only ones with good marriages, am I right?"

"Apparently not," Jennifer said.

"And you gotta admit that surprises you."

"OK, maybe. But I'll tell you one thing: if your marriage is as good as it appears, I'll bet you're living under God's principles whether you know it or not."

"How would we know? We're basically humanists. She more than I."

"Let me guess. I'll bet you're faithful to her and always have been."

Leo reddened. "It's only fair. We promised each other that, and I know she's upheld her end of the bargain. That's why I do."

"That's the only reason?"

He fidgeted. "You know, I don't have to tell you—"

"I know, Leo, and I'm sorry. That was too forward."

"That's OK, as long as you realize it. Another reason I'm faithful to her is because I love her, and I always have."

"That's a biblical principle that works for you."

"We aren't faithful because we think God wants us to be. We hardly believe in God. She doesn't at all."

"But you do?"

"Sometimes. He fits my politics."

"And I'll bet you don't go to sleep angry with each other."

Leo looked at her, surprised. "That's true," he said slowly. "How would you have guessed that?"

"Another biblical principle that makes for good marriages."

"It's not because it's a biblical principle," he said, growing louder. "It's just that neither of us likes any tension hanging in the air, so we compete to see who can get the thing straightened out first. It works for us."

"God doesn't require pure motives for His principles to work. They work no matter who uses them."

"Lucky for us," Leo said with an inflection that signaled the end of the conversation. Jennifer had felt more freedom in that discussion with him than ever before. She was glad she and Jim had visited their home. Maybe that had made it easier.

Four Fridays later, Jennifer had noticed Leo outside her glassed-in office visiting the newsroom. As a reporter said something that made him laugh, he was paged to the telephone.

Leo's face lost its color and he hurried to a phone. Jennifer stood and moved to her door. Just as Leo slammed down the phone and jogged to the elevator, his face taut, she stepped out and grabbed Neil Scotto, the scurrying young reporter, on his way out.

"No time, Jenn," he said. "Got a possible death in West Town."

She held his arm firmly. "Is that what you told Leo?"

"Yeah!" he said, pulling away. "I said it couldn't be him 'cause he was here. He said somethin' about nothing would surprise him in that neighborhood anymore. Jenn, I gotta go."

"Where's your car, Neil?"

"In back," he called over his shoulder.

"Pick me up out front," she said. "I'm coming with you."

He looked annoyed, but she knew he'd pull around and wait for her. She gathered up her bag and threw her coat over her shoulder. On her way out through the lobby she paused just long enough to ask the receptionist, "Who was that calling for Mr. Stanton?"

"A neighbor. Some kind of emergency."

# Two

Jennifer had waited at the curb on Michigan Avenue for less than a minute when Neil screeched up and popped open the passenger door from the inside.

"Where you been?" Jennifer kidded him as the skinny, goateed reporter wheeled back into the traffic.

"Funny," he said. "I know we have to cater to you hotshot privileged columnist types, but what makes you want to ride along on a police call? Miss the old beat?"

"Sometimes. What's the call?"

"Lady saw her next door neighbor's car in the garage later than usual. She wasn't worried. Figured she'd taken the day off. Wanted some company, gave her a call, no answer. Went over. Door was open, woman on her bed upstairs. Couldn't wake her."

"Dead?"

"Who knows?"

"That's Leo's neighborhood, you know."

"Yeah, that's why I said somethin' to him. He laughed."

"He's not laughing now. He got paged. The look on his face could have made me believe in premonitions, Neil. And after he took the call, he went past without even acknowledging me."

"Doesn't have to mean anything, Jennifer. Not everyone bows before your altar on their way out of the city room."

She ignored his crack. "The receptionist said his call was from a neighbor. I don't like it."

Neil fell silent. "I don't either," he said finally. "We'll know soon enough."

Jennifer was amazed at how different the neighborhood looked in the daytime. The lawns seemed brighter, the alleys grimier, the houses smaller and closer together. Her mind raced as they neared Leo's home.

She began to speak, but Neil shushed her with a gesture. He was listening intently to the squawking from his police radio scanner when Jennifer heard the familiar address.

"Neil, that's Leo's house," she said quickly. "Is that where we're going?"

He nodded ominously, the humor gone. "That's where we're going."

Police had already cordoned off the house, and Neil had to park half a block away. Dozens of neighbors crowded the scene, pushing at the edges of the area.

A paramedic vehicle had backed into the Stanton driveway. Neil was still trying to talk his way past the police lines when Jennifer found Steve Jeski, an old cop she knew from her police beat days, and was escorted in the side door.

"So what's the deal, Steve?" she asked. "I understand she didn't answer the door."

"She's dead, Jenn," the veteran said. "Suicide."

Jennifer wondered if she'd heard him right. "Surely not," she said. "I knew this woman, Steve. No way."

He motioned for her to follow. "You ain't got a camera, right?"

She nodded.

He led her in through the kitchen, down the hall, and up one flight of stairs. Other officers leaned against the wall in the hall, giving Officer Jeski dirty looks as he and Jennifer picked their way through to the bedroom.

"Whadya need, Steve?" the officer in charge, a Lieutenant Theodore Crichton, asked as they approached the door.

"Just a peek," he said, nodding at Jennifer.

Crichton recognized her. "No pictures," he said. They both nodded. Steve stepped back so Jennifer could peer in.

"Steve, she doesn't even look dead," she said, without turning around. "Are you sure?"

"She's dead all right, ma'am," a paramedic said. "Excuse me."

He and his partner edged past her, wheeling a litter into the room. Samantha Stanton lay on her side on her bed. The bed had been made, and she was fully dressed and made up, including jewelry, as if for work.

It appeared she had perhaps stretched out to relax a moment. Her face was nestled in one hand and she looked peaceful.

Jennifer took a quick peek back over her shoulder at the officers huddling in the hall and leaned into the room. "What was the cause of death?" she whispered.

"Self-inflicted poison," a paramedic said.

"How do you know that?" she asked, insistently.

"They told us," one said, pointing a thumb into the hall.

"*They* told *you*?" she asked. "Aren't *you* supposed to tell *them?*"

The medic picked up Mrs. Stanton's purse and tossed it to Jennifer, who had the presence of mind to jump out of the way and let it fall to the floor. "You shouldn't be touching anying in this room that you don't have to!" she scolded, nearly shouting. "You may not know it, but this is a crime scene."

"This is a suicide," he said.

"Suicide is a crime too. Don't touch anything more! Didn't you even try to revive her?"

"Sure we did! Hey, who do you think you are anyway?"

"Shut up," his partner said. "She's a reporter."

"Then get out," the first said.

"I want to know how you could have tried to revive her in the position she's in."

The police photographer entered. "Everybody out," he barked. Jennifer glared at the paramedics as she moved into the hall. "She back into the position you found her?" the photographer asked.

They nodded.

Jennifer stuck her head back in. "You're shooting a re-created scene?"

"Who's askin'?"

"Jennifer Grey, *Chicago Day*" she said.

"Talk to public relations downtown," he said. "I don't have to talk to you. In fact, I'm not s'posed to."

"I just want to know if you're shooting the body the way it was found."

"Yeah, sure."

"How do you know?"

"Cause the paramedics got no reason to lie."

"But they tried to revive her?"

"Course."

"Not in that position they didn't."

"Right again, Brenda Starr. You want a nice eight by ten glossy of this dame, or what?"

"So the paramedics worked on her and then put her back in the position they think they found her?"

"Somethin' wrong with that? Should they have waited till I got here for a few snap shots before they tried revivin' her, or what?"

"Leave 'im alone, Miss Grey," Lieutenant Crichton said, touching her shoulder. "He's just doing what he's told."

"Your crime scene is being destroyed," she said. "One of the paramedics grabbed her purse with his bare hand."

"I've already looked in her purse," the lieutenant said. "That's how we know it uas suicide."

"Your own men and the medics have contaminated the crime scene!"

"Nobody's contaminated nothin'," he said, pointing at the floor where the contents of Mrs. Stanton's purse had spilled.

Jennifer stared in disbelief at five booklets on suicide that had slid from Samantha's purse. She quickly scribbled their titles and publishers into her notebook as she heard commotion outside. Several officers bounded down the stairs to quell the disturbance. She moved to a window from which she could see Leo fighting to get into the house.

"Let me tell you something, Lieutenant," she said, surprised at her own bravado. "This woman's husband is Managing Editor of the *Day* and he'll find a way in here soon enough. There'd better be no more messing up of this scene than there's already been, or a lot of people here are going to be in big trouble."

Crichton screwed his face into a dirty look but stuffed the suicide booklets back into the purse himself. "Jeski!" he hollered, putting the purse back next to the bed where it had been discovered. "Get down there and tell them to let the husband in!"

He shooed the photographer and the paramedics from the room and pulled the door shut. When Leo reached the top of the stairs, huffing and puffing, he saw Jennifer and the lieutenant and slowed to a stop.

Jennifer burst into tears at the sight of him, and the desperately angry look on his face melted into disbelief "Jenn?" he said pitifully, asking the question without saying the words.

She nodded.

"I want to see her."

"You won't touch anything, sir?" the lieutenant asked.

He shook his head, and Crichton slowly opened the door. Leo knelt by the bed and impulsively felt Samantha's wrist for a heartbeat. He buried his face in her neck, and his sobs turned into a mournful, muffled wail that sliced through Jennifer like a winter wind.

She was tempted to make a deal with Lieutenant Crichton. The negotiation actually entered her mind, but she couldn't bring herself to broach the subject with him. It went against everything she believed in, and yet, in this case, she could have almost justified it.

She wanted to agree not to write about all the obvious errors in judgment and the sloppy evidence-gathering techniques during the last few minutes if he would agree to withhold from the other newspapers the discovery of the suicide booklets until the true cause of death had been determined.

But too many people already knew about the literature. Hiding it would be impossible—and unethical. Not writing about the shoddy police work would be wrong as well.

Her motive had been to protect Leo from embarrassment, she knew. Good motive, bad solution. She felt ashamed. The death *was* apparently a suicide. But how in the world would they ever know, the way the scene had been violated?

That night in Leo's home, she and Jim and Max Cooper and Assistant Managing Editor Ken Roloff sat with the stunned widower and gently urged him to make funeral plans. He had spent much of the day on the phone to relatives, but he couldn't bring himself to talk about the cause of death.

"I don't know what we can do about it in the *Day* Leo," Roloff whined, tugging at his over-the calf stockings and twitching his narrow shoulders, as was his custom. He pushed his wire-rimmed glasses closer to his eyes with one finger and, in the same motion, dragged his hand back through his thinning hair.

He was wearing the threadbare gray plaid suit he wore nearly every other day, an ensemble that didn't seem befitting of a man who had enjoyed the same responsible and profitable position for more than a decade.

Max Cooper, ever in character, stood and pushed his pointy tongue out the edge of his mouth and swore. His white, bushy eyebrows set off the red face and jaunty, thick little body that always seemed ready for action. "Of course you know what we can do about it, K.P! It gets listed as a death of undetermined causes."

Leo shook his head. "That won't solve anything," he said weakly, as if drained of life himself "Everybody knows that means suicide. Anyway, who's going to get the *Trib* or the *Times* to-call it unknown causes?"

He buried his head in his hands and cried anew. By mid-evening the funeral arrangements had been set. "Just family and close friends," Leo repeated often. "No press outside the *Day.*"

"That doesn't sound like you," Roloff said, slapping Leo on the back.

"It does too," he said flatly. "I was never one for covering funerals, not even of mobsters. You know that. You tried to get me to cover enough of 'em. Made me cover a few."

"Can't make you do anything now, can I?" Roloff said, smiling sympathetically.

Cooper swore again. "You're unbelievable, Kent, you know that? You think it makes Leo feel good to be reminded that he's your boss now? That really makes everything all right, doesn't it? You ever stop to think that maybe your lack of tact is the reason you've been stuck in the same job for years?"

Roloff was embarrassed. "I, I didn't mean anything, Mr. Cooper. I—"

"I know!" Cooper thundered. "You never—"

"Hey," Leo said, smiling and reaching out with both hands to the squabblers. "Can you guys fight somewhere else?"

"I'm sorry, Leo," Roloff said. Cooper stomped off.

"I want this thing covered in the *Day* the same way it'll be covered in the other two papers," Leo said.

Cooper came back in an arguing mood. "It's my paper," he said. "If I wanna protect my editor and his family, I can, can't I?"

"You can, Max, and I appreciate it," Leo said. "I really do. I don't believe Sam would have taken her own life any more than any of you do, I hope. In fact, I know better than any of you that she couldn't have. But if this happened to the wife of the editor of one of our competitors, I know we would cover it straight. We'd call it an apparent suicide, because that's what it is."

"You believe that?" Jennifer asked.

"I believe it's apparent," Leo said. "I just know that what's apparent is not what is true. But there's only one way to cover it. The truth will come out eventually. My family and I will survive."

Jennifer wasn't so sure. She pulled Mr. Cooper aside and told him she wanted to write the story in her column. He scowled and shook his head. "I don't think so," he said. "I don't think Leo'd go for it."

"I think he might," she countered.

"Then I won't go for it," he said. "Clear?"

"Why?"

"I don't need to tell you why, young lady, but I will. Your coverage will impugn the police department, which may have to be done anyway. But it will carry the bias of a personal friend and employee who doesn't believe what happened here any more than the grieving husband does. You're stunned. We're all stunned. Let the reporter—what's-his-name—handle it."

"Neil."

"Yeah, Scotto. It's the only way, Mrs. Grey. You're usually able to stay away from sentiment, but how could you here? It's not worth a column, outside of the fact that you work for the man and you knew them both. Am I right?"

Jennifer nodded, disappointed. "Would you give me a short leave of absence?"

"For what?"

"To check this thing out. The coroner ruled it a suicide because of the books the police found and the poison he found in her system. The autopsy will find nothing else, and that'll be the end of it. You can't let Leo investigate it. He's not up to it, and hell make himself miserable."

"He's already asked for some time off himself. I hope it's so he can rest at his Wisconsin place."

"Maybe if you told him I was going to check it out, he'd be able to rest. Otherwise he won't. When the shock wears off, if it ever does, he's going to want to get to the bottom of this. No matter what."

"And what if you find that it was suicide, Mrs. Grey? We never know the private torment many people carry in their minds."

"Then I'd have to think that would at least satisfy Leo. He'd want to know the truth, either way."

# Three

The Saturday morning papers, all three major dailies, carried the stark story of the apparent suicide of the wife of a prominent editor.

The *Day* also carried a note that columnist Jennifer Grey would be on assignment for approximately two weeks.

In truth, she had been granted a leave of absence for not longer than three weeks.

Jennifer and Jim had invited Leo to church on Sunday, the day before the funeral, and he had almost accepted. "Good strategy," he had said wryly. "Catch me at a vulnerable time." But his family had flown in, and he would be at the funeral home all day.

Family, close friends, and no press except the Day turned out to be about three hundred people. The Monday morning funeral became more of an ordeal than Leo expected. He had to be supported as he walked from the car to the grave site.

His older child, Mark, arranged to be away from his own business for a week and was set to go through his mother's things with Leo and then spend a few days at the Wisconsin cottage with him. Jennifer was glad Leo could get away and have company, but she wanted to talk to him first, if he was up to it.

Tuesday evening, when only Leo and Mark were in the house and Jim was on duty, she visited. Mark, a tall, brooding, darkly handsome man in his late twenties, sat in on the conversation but said nothing to Jennifer. He'd been away from home for many years, but it was apparent he knew his father.

Whenever Leo seemed to be losing control, when his breath came in short spurts and his lips quivered, Mark would change the subject or bring him something to drink. More than once, Jennifer got the impression that Mark felt she was intruding, that everything was happening too quickly, that his father needed time to himself to deal with his grief and put it behind him.

But Leo persuaded her otherwise. "I need you to do this for me, Jenn," he said, his voice breaking. "I appreciate it more than you know. I wish I could help with strategy, but I can't think. You know what I mean."

"Of course, Leo. You want to know where I'm going to start?"

He nodded.

"I've gotten copies of the literature that your wife had in her purse."

"That was *planted* in her purse you mean," he said quickly. "That's the farthest thing from what Sam would have chosen to read, isn't it, Mark? Show her what your mother liked to read."

Mark produced books on art and literature and, of course, geography and travel. Jennifer nodded and smiled.

"Still I feel it's important to know what those booklets are all about, don't you, Leo?"

He nodded again. "I'd like to see 'em myself."

Jennifer had them in her handbag, but she hesitated. Mark spoke up. "No, you wouldn't, Dad," he said firmly. "Maybe someday. Not now."

"Why not?"

"Trust me, Dad. Not now, all right?"

Leo smiled and clapped a hand on his son's thigh. "All right, big guy. All right."

Jennifer was relieved. She hadn't had a chance to read through them herself, but she knew they were nothing for a grieving man to see.

"I couldn't sleep in our bed," Leo said suddenly, quietly.

"I can imagine," Jennifer said, fighting tears herself.

"No, you can't, but thanks for saying so."

"Leo," she said, hoping the sound of her voice would remind him that she certainly could imagine, that she too had lost a spouse, that she could remember all too well the haunting emptiness of a bed that threatened to swallow her if she dared sleep in it alone. Even in his grief she couldn't permit him to pretend that he was the only one who had suffered this kind of grief, especially not in front of a fellow sufferer.

He looked up at her sadly. "Jennifer, forgive me," he said. "I know you know. I remembered when you didn't try to say all the things everyone else tried to say."

Mark glared down at her. She stood. "I'd better go, Leo," she said. "I'll see you again whenever you say."

"No!" he said, desperate and suddenly lucid. "I want to know what you're going to do and how you're going to do it. I can't think clearly right now, but maybe if I know what you're up to, I'll think of something that'll help. Samantha didn't kill herself, Jennifer. You know that. And even if you don't, I do. If anybody can find the truth, you can."

He was crying again. "Leo," she said, softly, "you're not ready for this, are you? Let's talk again tomorrow, OK? I'll see you in the afternoon after I've talked to the coroner and the police and the woman next door."

He nodded, his head in his hands.

Mark helped her with her coat and walked her to the front door. "Thanks for being sensitive," he said. "You're very special to him."

Jennifer was surprised. If anything, she had expected a lecture from the stern-faced son. In the light from the porch she could see that he was smiling a grateful smile at her. And he opened the door, gently guiding her through it with a hand on her arm.

He let his hand slide down into her gloved fingers, which he squeezed briefly while thanking her. "We'll see you tomorrow," he said.

Jennifer lay in bed till two in the morning reading the short booklets. They were as scary and bizarre as anything she had ever read, not because they were horrifying or macabre. Rather because they were so reasoned, so deftly crafted, so persuasive.

The first made the clear point that the only prospect worse than an unacceptable life was a failed effort to terminate it. The book was the text for a euthanasia society that had nearly ten thousand members, all dedicated to the lofty ideal that they would rather take their own lives in relative peace and gentleness than to suffer a horrible end while enduring the ravages of disease.

The justification was on the basis of the reluctance of the dying to become burdens on their families or to suffer unduly themselves when the results would be the same regardless. They were going to die, so they wanted a hand in it.

Of course, the philosophy centered on the assumption that death was the total end of life. That's why the booklets, as genteel and slick as they were, stuck in Jennifer's craw. Because she believed that God was the author of life and that it was His to give or to take, euthanasia, regardless of the wrappings, was unacceptable.

Another booklet extolled the virtues of peaceful death, making it sound not only soothing, but desirable. Jennifer wondered what that might mean to those who weren't pain-wracked by disease or so old that they would rather be gone. She disagreed with suicide in any case, but making it so easy might tempt people who had even shallower reasons to consider it.

Everything she read pointed to suicide as an escape. There was no compulsion to face life head-on or to seek God or to serve others. One booklet referred to "assisted suicide" as the "compassionate crime."

*Assisted suicide*, Jennifer thought. *I wonder what my homicide detective friends would call that?*

Another booklet presented the case for dual suicides and called self-inflicted death "self-deliverance." Jennifer shuddered. The language and the logic was not unlike what she had read in sales pitches for retirement villages in Florida.

One of the guides justified itself by hoping that it would aid in cutting down the incidences of botched suicide attempts. While making the case that suicide should be a last resort—at least a moderate approach compared to the others—it went on to prescribe specific doses of drug combinations that would result in deaths so peaceful that the body looks dead, but not disgusting.

Jennifer couldn't help but think of how Mrs. Stanton had looked on Friday morning. She would ask Jake Steinmetz, the Cook County Coroner, about the drugs found in the body.

Early the next morning, Jennifer visited the University of Chicago Law School library where she learned that in England it is a crime to aid a would-be suicide. In the U.S., she discovered, suicide, and even attempted suicide, are ironically punishable crimes and that assisting a suicide is also illegal.

She asked a law student, "If it's illegal to aid a suicidal person in his effort, why can this material be printed and sold?"

"You ought to know that, if you're who I think you are," he said. "The First Amendment guarantees that you can write and publish anything you want. And so can the euthanasiasts. Don't threaten their freedom unless you're willing to have yours threatened as well. There are plenty of books available on how to lie, cheat, steal, and even murder."

Jake Steinmetz was, as always, pleased to find a few moments for his favorite newspaper reporter. They had worked together many times in the past. He was shocked when she guessed the precise dosage of drugs found in Mrs. Stanton's system.

"Jennifer, I'm afraid I'm going to have to remind you that I am a friend of the court."

"What do you mean by that?"

"Just that I'm sure that your boss has not been entirely ruled out as a suspect, and if you somehow know the dosage well, that can't look terribly good for him. I would only be doing my duty to report it."

"Jake, my boss would love nothing more than to think that this case was shifting in suspicion from a suicide to a homicide. Please tell me you'll do that, put him under suspicion, get them to admit that this could have been a murder."

Steinmetz smiled his knowing smile. "You set me up," he said. "All I was fishing for was how you knew the dosage. The cops aren't at liberty to release that yet."

"I read it in a book, OK?"

"How did you know about the books?"

"I work hard, Jake. Just like you do. I do my homework. I have sources. Anyway, I was there."

"I won't pursue that, Jennifer."

"Thanks."

"I'm satisfied it was a suicide."

"Apparently for the same reason I'm convinced it wasn't," she said.

"How's that?"

"Because the dosage matches the prescription in the book."

"That's right."

"Why not prove it?"

"We already know it, Jennifer. It's proven."

"I mean prove the drugs were purchased by Mrs. Stanton. That should be easy enough. Wouldn't a pharmacist recall selling her lethal dosages?"

"No pharmacist in his right mind would fill a prescription like that."

"Then where would she get it, assuming she got it?"

"Probably from two different druggists. The ingredients are not alarming in themselves. Only when mixed do they result in the deep, peaceful sleep."

"That results in death."

"Precisely."

"That should be easy enough to check too," Jennifer said. "How many pharmacists are there in the area?"

"Hundreds. Be my guest."

"I just might."

"You probably will. That's what I admire about you, Jennifer. Naturally, if anything turns up, I'll be eager to hear about it."

"Naturally. But you want me to do the legwork."

"Right again. As I said, I'm—"

"Satisfied. Yeah, I know. At least tell me how she ingested the dosage."

"With water."

"You're sure? It wasn't mixed with her food or dropped in her orange juice?"

"You're impugning your boss again, Jennifer."

"I am not! Please quit saying that. If there's one thing I'm certain of, it's that Leo had nothing to do with his wife's death. I have to think someone poisoned her. If so, how would they have done it?"

"The autopsy showed a light breakfast and residue of an extremely fast dissolving mixture of the lethal chemicals, possibly in tablet form, but more likely mixed in water."

"You're guessing."

"Yes, I'm guessing she mixed it in water."

"Why? To fit your suicide theory? Where are the prescription bottles? The spoon? The water glass? Would there not be residue on her water glass?"

"There was none. That's why I said possibly in tablet form."

"You said it was more likely mixed in water. Why would she have been careful to clean the glass? Would she have had time?"

"Barely. She would have grown heavily drowsy almost immediately."

"She took it in tablet form, Jake."

"So?"

"One tablet she made up herself? No one would sell her that small a quantity of each ingredient, so where is the rest?"

"I don't know, Jennifer. This is your fairy tale, not mine."

"Did you check any medicine bottles in her purse?"

"Of course, but this is totally off-the-record, Jennifer. No one has this. You can't print it yet."

She raised her eyebrows. "Deal," she said.

"There was a bottle of plain, white aspirin tablets, the large type you take one at a time."

"And?"

"Microscopic residue of the poisonous mixture on one of the tablets. Not enough to hurt a flea."

Jennifer leaned forward in her chair. "Jake! That means the death tablet could have been in that bottle, doesn't it?"

"What if it was?"

"Then it could have been planted!"

He shrugged and raised his hands in protest. "Could have, could have," he repeated, as if she were dreaming.

"There was no suicide note, Jake. How often does that occur?"

"I don't concern myself with suicide notes."

"You never let a note help you determine a suicide?"

"Well, sure, I mean, sometimes it's obvious, and the note confirms it, and—"

"The woman was dressed for work, Jake. She had eaten a light breakfast. Don't you sometimes have to wonder why someone kills herself without a hint of the normal suicide pattern or even a reason?"

"Sometimes."

"This time, Jake."

"Happy hunting, Jennifer."

# Four

"Are we off-the-record, Miss Grey?" Lieutenant Crichton asked, leaning back in his chair with his hands behind his head. She nodded. "I've got to tell you I was on pins and needles all weekend waiting for your story to take us apart."

"It could have."

"Of course it could have. I'm fully aware of that. You were right. Why didn't you print what you saw?"

"I'm not on the story. Too close to it. Leo Stanton is my boss, and I knew his wife. The guy who's covering it, Neil Scotto, didn't see what I saw."

"I'm glad, because we almost blew it."

"Almost?" she said.

"You don't still think this was other than a suicide, do you?"

"I do."

He shook his head slowly. "Well, I feel some obligation to you for not making us look bad. We did a lot of things wrong, I'll admit that. But not publicly. I'm still convinced it was a suicide. But if there's anyway I can help you, let me know."

"Did you check it out, Lieutenant, or are you basing everything on what you found in her purse?"

"We checked her out some. You know, her interests and politics point to this sort of, ah, liberal, um, mercy-killing type of thing."

"Euthanasia?"

"Right. She could have easily been into that."

"But was she? Do you have any evidence that she belonged to any such group or was on any mailing list?"

He shook his head. "That would require a lot of man hours, and the coroner is satisfied that it was suicide."

"But how about drugstores? Wouldn't it pay to find out where she got the ingredients?"

"We don't think so. I'm sorry. We just don't."

"Yet you're willing to help me?"

"Sure, what can I offer?"

"Put Cap Duffy on this case."

"Duffy? The homicide detective? I can't do that."

"Why not?"

"First of all, I'm not in homicide. I can't go assigning their people. Second, if I *were* in homicide, I wouldn't put a homicide guy on a suicide."

"Then what do you mean when you say you owe me, you're obligated to me, you want to help me? How can you do anything for me if you can't help me prove this wasn't a suicide?"

"You're gonna have to prove that on your own."

"So you're not really willing to help me. You just appreciate that I didn't blow the whistle on your sloppy work at the scene of the crime."

"At the scene of the death. When I offered to help you, I was thinking in terms of any driving or parking violations that you'd like me to investigate for you. Perhaps something I could check into more carefully than the arresting officer did."

"Wonderful. You want to fix a ticket for me."

"Oh, my—no, ma'am. I would never do something like that. However, I do have the power to interrupt the judicial process on certain violations if my investigation turns up mitigating circumstances, if you know what I mean."

"I know what you mean. Fortunately, I don't speed, and the *Day* pays my parking tickets."

"That is fortunate."

"Yeah, for you too."

"Me?"

"You just offered to fix a ticket. I could get you in big trouble."

"I would never do anything of the sort. Maybe you have friends or relatives or acquaintances who might like to take their kids to the circus, but who can't afford it."

Jennifer stood. "Tell me you're kidding. You want to thank me for not writing the truth, which was hardly as a favor to you. And you want to show your appreciation by compounding the problem? No, sir! It's a wonder any crime gets solved in this city."

Crichton smiled condescendingly. "If I weren't still afraid you might point your poison pen at us, I'd warn you that a remark like that could result in your hoping you never do get a ticket in my precinct."

Jennifer left without another word, more determined than ever to find out the truth on her own. She might seek Jim's counsel, but she couldn't involve him in the investigation.

Just after lunch she pulled into the driveway next to Leo's house. It appeared his car was gone. She hoped Mark had taken him out to lunch.

Mrs. Wilma Fritzee, Leo's neighbor to the south, was a lonely, talkative, sixty-fiveyear-old widow of nearly a decade who carried her age well. She fussed over Jennifer, bringing her tea and cookies and leading a tour of the house.

"I know what it's like for Leo," she said. "The suddenness of it and everything. Edgar was older than I was, you know. Ten years. Retired from the foundry not three months. Died on our way to Florida for the big vacation we'd saved years for."

"I'm sorry. I lost my first husband too."

"Oh, my. And so young. But you're married again?"

"No, I shouldn't have said first husband. My only husband. I'm engaged."

"How wonderful! I was almost engaged again myself, but I'm afraid my new man thought I had more money than I did. When he checked into that, he lost interest."

"I'll bet you're glad of that."

"Oh, in the long run I am. Who wants a man who marries for money? I always thought it was women who did that, but you know, I'd never do that. There are days, though, when I could go crazy without someone to talk to, and I wonder if the loneliness is worth it."

"Worth the principle you mean?"

But Wilma Fritzee was lost in thought. Her eyes glazed over. "Samantha was good to me," she said. "I can hardly believe she's gone. I would listen for her car leaving just before eight-thirty every morning, and I don't mind telling you I was always just a little disappointed when she left. She owns that company, you know, and she could pretty much come and go as she pleased."

"And sometimes she didn't go to work?" Jennifer asked.

"Sometimes. Not very often. Usually she was out of there like clockwork. Leo—Mr. Stanton—he always left pretty early in that little car of his. 'Course he never misses work unless he's on his deathbed—oh, excuse me, I didn't mean to say it that way, but you know what I mean. Of course, you work for the man, so you know exactly what I mean."

Jennifer nodded.

"But every once in a while, after Mrs. Stanton—Sam I always called her, it was all right with her—after she'd been on one of those one- or two week trips to who knows where, she might be home a day or two the next week."

"Resting up from the trip?"

"Well, I guess so, but you know, it was never the first day or two after she got back because I guess she had to go into the office and get back on track or something. But after the trip and then after she'd been in the office a day or two, it would be like she wanted to wind down or take a break or something. That's when I would listen and hope I wouldn't hear that car of hers leaving the driveway."

"And if it didn't?"

"I'd get right on the phone to her."

"Weren't you afraid of disturbing her so early?"

"Oh, I'd look for the paper first. Leo, he leaves the morning paper for her because I imagine he gets one free at the office. If the paper was still out there, I'd leave her alone. But if it was gone, I'd know she's up. Know what? She usually was too."

"Was what?"

"Up early, even on the days she took off. That's the kind of a woman she was. I loved her. Always have. Did anyway. It would make me so sad to think she really, you know, did it herself. I can't believe there could have been that much going on inside her head without me knowing about it."

"You were that close?"

"We're the only two houses on this block that still have the same people in 'em for thirty years. We've been here since long before Leo and Sam moved in, honest. I remember when they moved in. Didn't even have kids then. Remember the kids bein' born, babysittin' 'em. Never had an argument all these years, though I used to get after those kids when they were little. But Sam didn't mind. She told me to holler at 'em if they were into somethin' they shouldn't be. What was your question?"

"I was just wondering if you were really close enough to know whether she was having some real difficulty, either physically or mentally."

"I don't know. Maybe not. I know she just has tolerated me for the last several years since Ed's been gone. Not that we did much together as couples. Just a few cookouts each year, and Leo and Ed might sit out in the yard with a beer and watch a ball game on the portable."

"Why do you think she was just tolerating you?"

"Well, because I was always the one to call her. She'd never call me first. And I don't blame her. Heaven knows I never gave her the chance. If her car was in and her paper gone by eight-thirty, ol' Wilma was on the horn. Never gave her much chance to even read the paper, I don't s'pose."

"Did she ever make you feel like you were intruding?"

Mrs. Fritzee stood and moved toward the large picture window in her living room and leaned over the couch to peer out past the shared driveway into the front yard of the Stanton home. She took a deep breath

and let out a rattling sigh. Her voice was thick with emotion when she spoke again.

"No," she said, straightening but not turning around. "She never once made me feel anything less than a million bucks. Her and Leo both. Treated Edgar the same way. We talked about that nearly every day of our married lives, I'll tell you that. Here was a foundry worker and a housewife. I never worked. Ed wouldn't have it. We suffered for it, but I wouldn't trade—"

Her voice trailed off as she remembered her other loss. But when she was ready, she picked up right where she had left off. "Here was Leo, always a big shot with the newspapers. You know, before they started this new one you work for, there was five of 'em there for a while. Seems there was more than that years ago, maybe seven.

"But Leo was always right in the middle of one of 'em, bein' the number one guy in some section or another. Always movin' up. And Sam, she was makin' money from day one in that travel agency as soon as her kids was in high school; it had to been before Edgar died when she bought into the company. She's the only owner who works there, you know."

"I didn't know that."

"Oh, yeah. I think there's four other owners, something like that. But she owns half of it and runs it. I guess. I don't really know. That's sorta how it is. How it was, I mean. I don't know what happens now. Do you?"

Jennifer shook her head. Mrs. Fritzee seemed almost embarrassed, as if she suddenly realized that she was standing nearly in another room, forcing herself to talk loud enough for Jennifer to hear.

She shuffled back over and sat heavily, covered her mouth with an open palm, and let it slide down her chin. "I was tellin' you what Ed and I used to say about them, wasn't I?"

Jennifer nodded.

"It was just that they always seemed to do good. Leo I'm sure was makin' OK money, and Sam did at least that good. They always had everything they needed and wanted, and they dressed well, traveled a lot, that type of thing.

"Edgar was a good worker, but there was never any money for him at the foundry. In forty-five years he worked up to quality control inspector and was shop union steward. We saved for that Florida trip for years and years, and the farthest we ever got away from here before that was a train ride to my sister's in New Mexico. We knew who we were and who we weren't, and we were happy, you understand."

"I sure do."

"You have children, young lady?"

"No, ma'am."

"That's good. I mean, that's good that they wasn't left without a father, you know what I mean? Only grief we ever had was our two boys. Neither one of 'em have amounted to much, but at least Edgar never really knew that. Both of 'em have kids their wives won't let 'em see. Pitiful."

Jennifer silently agreed. Here was a lonely old woman with no-account sons who just lost the only apparent listener she had left in the world.

The old woman sighed again and seemed on the verge of tears. "I keep gettin' off the track," she said. "The thing that Ed and I used to always say about Sam and Leo was that they treated us like friends."

"Oh, I'm sure you *were* their friends, Mrs. Fritzee."

"I know, but not really. I mean, we never went anywhere with them. We couldn't really talk about their lives. But Leo knew how to get Ed talkin' about the foundry, and Sam always told me about where she'd been as if next time I went anywhere, that's where it would be. I'm not kidding. She'd say stuff like, 'You gotta watch it in the market there and make sure you get your best deal. Don't let 'em smooth talk you, Wilma,' she'd say. And I'd laugh, 'cause there was no way I was goin' to wherever she was talkin' about, but it was fun to pretend.

"There's enough snooty people in this neighborhood who got nothin' to be snooty about. And here was a couple who had every right to act above us all because they was—and yet they was good as gold."

She dabbed at her eyes with the end of her apron and stood again. "Do you know," she said, almost unable to speak, "if either of us was ever in the yard when Leo or Sam had some big shot over, they would introduce us."

"That's Leo," Jennifer agreed.

"Both of 'em!" Mrs. Fritzee corrected. "Sam too."

Jennifer nodded. And the old woman wept.

# Five

By the time Jennifer was able to pull away from Mrs. Fritzee, Leo's car was back in his garage.

"Dad has had a rough morning," Mark said, as Leo seemed to nap on the couch. Jennifer could tell Leo was wide awake, but he lay there on his side in casual clothes and stocking feet with his eyes closed.

Jennifer was struck by how much he looked like his wife in her last repose, but of course she couldn't comment on it.

"How rough?" she whispered.

"He just wanted to go to a park they used to visit. We strolled around awhile and then sat at their favorite picnic table. It wasn't easy for him. I hope it accomplished whatever he wanted it to. Strange though, I never went to that park before."

"Why is that strange?"

"I just meant that it was apparently a place they had discovered after my sister and I had left home."

"Wrong," Leo mumbled, eyes still closed. Mark and Jennifer jumped. Mark smiled.

"Wrong?"

"Wrong. It was where we went alone, even when you two were around."

"Hm. I feel left out."

"That was the point."

Mark laughed, apparently encouraged that his father's sense of humor was returning.

Leo sighed heavily and turned over, facing the back of the couch. "Shall we leave, Dad?" Mark asked.

Leo shook his head.

"Maybe talk in another room?" Mark suggested.

Leo shook his head again. "I like you right where you are." Soon he was breathing deeply, as if asleep.

"If he is, it's the first sound sleep he's gotten since Friday night," Mark said.

Jennifer grimaced in sympathy, but Leo stirred, and she wondered if he could sleep soundly even now.

"I need to talk to my fiancé and make several other calls anyway," she said. "Perhaps I should come back later."

"Oh, please stay," Mark said. "I enjoy your company." His direct gaze made her uncomfortable, and she couldn't return it, though she was flattered. "If Dad's not awake in an hour, I'll get him up with the smell of coffee and tuna fish, one of his favorite light meals. He hasn't eaten much."

"You don't think you should let him sleep?"

"Oh, sure, if the smell of coffee doesn't wake him, I won't push it."

"I needed to ask him about your mother's morning habits," she whispered, "and after talking to your neighbor, about the other partners in the travel agency too."

"Well, I wouldn't know anything about the agency. I never took much of an interest in that, though I was proud of Mom for jumping into it. It made me want to start my own business. Which I did."

"And which is?"

"Small sub-contracting firm. Plumbing and electrical. I know nothing of either one." He smiled.

"I'll bet," she said.

"Really! Well, just enough to keep my people honest. But my thing is business. I'd electrocute myself or drown if I started messing with the actual work."

Jennifer almost laughed, but she saw the same look come to Mark's face that came to Mrs. Fritzee's when she realized she had joked about death when everyone's grief was so fresh. She changed the subject quickly.

"You don't recall anything about your mother's morning habits."

"Not really. I suppose they're different now than they were when I was in high school. That was just before she started working. She was always a crack-of-dawn type. Up with Dad, breakfast for everybody but herself, then shooing us all out the door. Good mood in the morning. More than I can say for me or Dad."

"She didn't eat breakfast?"

"Oh, yeah, but it was sort of her reward when she had everybody out the door. She'd settle in at the dining room table with her newspaper and her toast and tea. And some kinda jam."

"Marmalade," Leo said.

With that, Mark stood and motioned for Jennifer to follow him to the kitchen. Leo grunted in protest when he realized they were leaving, but he stayed where he was and said nothing.

For half an hour or so, Mark and Jennifer sat across from each other at the kitchen table, chatting about everything except the Stantons. She told him about her husband, her home, her family, her job, and her fiancé.

Mark didn't appear to want to discuss Jim. Yes, he had met him at the funeral, but "of course you realize I wasn't thinking rationally. I'm still not. I noticed you though; I do recall that."

Jennifer didn't know what to say. "So, your father likes tuna sandwiches? I don't think I ever knew that."

"Only the way we make 'em here at home," Mark said, rising and expertly preparing a pot of coffee. He noticed Jennifer's surprise. "From years of living alone," he said. And she looked away.

He popped a can of tuna into the electric opener as if he'd done it every day of his life, picked the meat from the can with a fork and got every morsel, and mixed it in a plastic bowl with plenty of mayonnaise. Then he added diced onion, sweet and dill pickle, and celery.

"You like olives?" he asked, suddenly looking up.

She smiled and shook her head. "Not in tuna," she said.

"Shoot," he said. "I was looking for a reason for us to make a run to the store."

"You shouldn't leave Leo right now anyway, should you?" she asked, wishing she'd been bolder and just told him to back off. She was, after all, engaged, not available, off limits, not interested. Well, at least three out of four.

"I s'pose not," he said, rummaging around for a platter for the sandwiches and a bowl for chips. "You want Coke, milk, tea?"

"Coffee is fine," she said.

He placed everything in the middle of the kitchen table, and as if on cue, his father padded in from the living room. Noticing the table, Leo couldn't suppress a sad smile. "Always said you'd make somebody a fine wife someday."

Mark shook his head in mock frustration. "Sit down, you old coot."

Mark was pouring the coffee when his father surprised him. "I want Jennifer to say grace," he said, more as an announcement than as a request. "You mind, Mark.?"

His son was taken aback, but he just shrugged.

"Jennifer, would you?" Leo asked.

"Sure," she said, panicking. Wasn't it Leo who had advised her to quit praying over her meals at the office and with her colleagues? She had never prayed aloud, of course, but she had always felt she should just bow her head.

She had told Leo she didn't feel she was making a show of it, and he told her it made everyone uncomfortable. She asked a few friends, who agreed with Leo and who added that it seemed a little holier-than-thou.

She had even talked it over with her parents, who thought she should continue it as a witness. "You never know who might be affected by that little gesture," her father said.

But she had decided to stop doing it. She wasn't doing it for a witness, and she certainly didn't want to make a show of it, which was hard to avoid because people noticed, no matter how subtle she was.

It had been months since their discussion, and she had felt a little guilty about bailing out. But she had gotten over that. She and Jim prayed together, of course, and even at meals. And she prayed during her own time alone.

But now Leo wanted her to pray, aloud and in front of his son—a self—proclaimed humanist, basically agnostic, almost atheist—and himself, a basically patriotic rightwinger whose god was conservative politics and the free enterprise system.

She bowed her head and closed her eyes, her heart drumming. "Father God," she began, "thank You for Your love and for Your provision of food. Thank You for a family of people who care for each other. Be with them in their time of grief. In the name of Jesus Christ, Amen."

There was a moment of awkward silence before Leo reached for a sandwich. Though he didn't speak, it was obvious he was overcome with emotion. He fought tears and chewed slowly, as if not really hungry.

Mark ate quickly, nervously.

"Delicious," Jennifer said.

"Yeah, Mark. It's good," Leo said.

Mark nodded. He had quit staring into Jennifer's eyes, as he had done all afternoon. She decided that if her prayer had had no other effect than to put him off a little, that would be fine. And then, of course, she felt guilty for that.

Except for those brief compliments to the chef, they sat in silence. After a few minutes, less than half a sandwich, and one cup of coffee, Leo rose unsteadily and apologized.

He shuffled from the room with the fingers of his right hand pressed to his forehead. He peeked under his hand to see where to walk. Jennifer and Mark stood quickly and watched him amble back to the couch where he sat and cried, his head in his hands.

Suddenly, Jennifer wasn't hungry. Mark encouraged her to finish, but she couldn't. He wolfed another half sandwich and took his cup with him into the living room. Jennifer followed.

"Enough action for one day, Dad?" Mark said smiling. "Shall I kick her out or take her somewhere?"

Leo wiped his eyes and tried to force a smile. "I'd rather kick you out and let her stay," he said.

"This may not be the right thing to say, Leo," she said, "but it hurts me to see you hurt."

"I appreciate that," he managed. "I'm all right." He winked at Mark. "It's just that his mother made those sandwiches so much better than he can!"

"Ouch!" Mark said. "I thought they were particularly good."

"So did I," Jennifer said.

And the awkward silence returned. The sun was setting, and Mark stood to close the drapes. "Leave them open, if you don't mind," Leo said. He sat with his hands in his lap, his shoulders sagging, staring out into the twilight.

"You haven't seen me like this, have you, Jenn?" he said.

She shook her head, not able to speak.

"Big tough guy editor, never needs anything or anybody, right? That's me. I can hassle everybody, afraid of nobody. I'm champion of the old-fashioned cause. We do it right because that's the only way to do it. Credibility and trustworthiness and our reputation is all we have, right?"

Jennifer didn't know what he was driving at, but she nodded. It reminded her of his late-night harangues against sloppy journalism or management selling editorial out for the sake of an advertising dollar.

Leo would fight with anybody, even Max Cooper, over principle. And Leo usually won.

"But the only reason I could do that without fear," he was saying now, "is that I came home to the Rock of Gibraltar." His face contorted, and the tears flowed, but he made no move to hide them or wipe them away.

Jennifer impulsively sat next to him and put her arm around his shoulders. He sobbed.

She peeked at her watch. She would meet Jim in an hour, but she needed information from Leo first. She wanted to be clear on his wife's morning routine. She wanted to know of the other partners in the travel agency. And she wanted to know what drugstores the family frequented. But she didn't dare ask.

She tried another tack. "When are you heading for your cottage, Leo?"

He shrugged. "The sooner the better, I guess. Do you think I'm weak, Jennifer?"

"Leo, you're one of the strongest men I've ever known. You've meant more to me in my career than anyone. You're hurting and grieving, and you shouldn't fight that. Let it happen. If you weren't tender right now,

after a long and good marriage to a wonderful woman, I'd worry about you."

He nodded. "I'm not going to sleep tonight. I just know it. And I need to. I'm exhausted."

"You must be," she said. "Do you ever use sleeping pills?"

"Never have," he said, "but right now I'd be willing to try."

"Where would you get them?" she asked.

"I'd want a prescription," he said. "None of these over-the-counter things."

"I can call your doctor, Dad," Mark said. "You still see Billings?"

Leo nodded.

"What pharmacy do you use, Leo?" Jennifer asked as Mark went to the phone.

He thought a moment. "Hargreaves on Western," he said. "Or the one next to the grocery store on Kedzie."

When Mark returned, he told his father that Dr. Billings had advised against sleeping pills. "He said he'd be glad to prescribe valium—"

"No way!" Leo said, almost shouting. "I've read enough about that to know I wouldn't touch it. Forget it. I'll just ride this out."

"He also said that in case you were still as belligerent about valium as you were the last time he saw you—which, he wanted me to remind you, was more than eighteen months ago—a change of scenery might be the best medicine."

"You tell him we were going up to the cottage tomorrow?"

"Yeah. He said make it tonight."

"Tonight?"

"Tonight. He said you'd probably sleep in the car on the way up there, which would be good, even if you didn't sleep well once you got there."

"If I'm sleepin' when we get there, leave me in the car. When do we leave?"

Leo had so brightened at the prospect of the trip that Jennifer knew she could ask him what she needed to. "Why doesn't Mark pack a bag for you while you chat with me," she suggested. "Just give me enough to keep me going on this until you get back."

# Six

Leo painfully told Jennifer the mundane details of his wife's morning routine. For some reason he found it particularly difficult. Just thinking about her in her normal habits of life seemed almost too much for him.

Several times Jennifer offered to put it off till another time, but Leo wouldn't hear of it. "In the middle of this pain, I feel more strongly than ever the need to prove she didn't kill herself, Jennifer."

He told her his wife rose with him, made their breakfast, and just before her last cup of tea, she would finish dressing and making herself up for work. Then she would clear away the dishes, run upstairs for a final shot of mouth wash and some lipstick and peek in the mirror, and then head back downstairs to read her paper until it was time to leave.

The phone rang. It was Kent Roloff's wife. "Yeah, June, how ya doin'?" Leo asked. "Oh, I'm OK, thanks. It's not easy, June.... Yes, I know, it's hard on all of us. You were close, yes.... Twenty years? I wouldn't have guessed it was that long.... Well, I don't believe it either, but I'm working on that.... Yeah, Mark's running me up to the cottage for a few days.... Right, last summer.... Uh-huh, that was fun. Maybe we can do it again this year. You two and me anyway, I mean.... Oh, I'm sure Kent is taking care of everything for me. Tell him I appreciate it, if I don't get to talk with him.... Oh, he is? Well, all right.... Hi, Kent.... Yeah, I hope to see you next Monday.... No, I won't rush it. I'll let you know. Thanks for everything, buddy."

Leo hung up and rolled his eyes. "If the truth were known, I can hardly stomach the man," he said. "June's a doll, though. Always fun to be with. She and Sam were like sisters. This is as hard on June as it is on me."

"Surely not."

"Well, she thinks so. I don't think she has any idea. But they *were* close. June helped Sam in her travel class. She took the course and then served as sort of a volunteer aide. Did that for years. Could probably teach the course herself by now. And when Samantha won trips for two and I couldn't go, which was at least once a year and sometimes two, June

was always her first and only choice. Their friendship was developed around the world."

"She never took Mrs. Fritzee?"

"You know, she asked her once. June couldn't go for some reason, and Sam bucked up her courage and asked Wilma."

"Why did that take courage?"

"You've talked to the woman. Sam was afraid she'd talk all the way to Bangkok and back. Probably would have, too."

"Why didn't she go?"

"Didn't have a dime for clothes or souvenirs or incidentals, and Sam didn't want to offend her by offering to give her cash too, though she would have been happy to pay for the companionship. Sam was really quite relieved when Wilma said no. She wound up taking one of the gals from the office."

"Do you feel up to telling me about her business, Leo?"

"Yeah. She owned half of it, and there are four other shares at twelve and a half percent each."

"Who owns them?"

"I hardly know. One's an investment banker who just sees it as a good investment. There's a retired couple in Texas who own a piece. And then there's a holding company of some kind—it's got initials in its name—that owns the two other shares."

"Is it worth checking into, Leo?"

"What—the ownership? Aw, I doubt it. They're mostly friendly. They have semi-annual meetings where the couple from Texas, the banker from downtown, and a local lawyer representing the holding company meet with Samantha. Guess I'll have to get involved in all that baloney now. She left me forty percent of the company."

"Only forty? That means you still have controlling stock by quite a significant margin. But if that holding company buys one of the other small shares out, you'd only have a small edge on them."

"Good grief, Jennifer, I could hardly care less. I'd be happy to sell it out to them myself."

"Do you mind telling me who your wife left her other ten percent of the company to?"

"Not at all—it was a wonderful gesture. Just a little nest egg for June Roloff."

"That was a nice thought, Leo. But do you see how it threatens your control of the company?"

"I suppose, but I'd always have June in my corner, so there's no way anyone can get more than fifty percent. In that sense, it's just like it's always been. I'll wind up splitting my shares between my kids someday

anyway. Problem is—unless I sell, which I really shouldn't—I have to be chairman of that fool board. Major stockholder gets that dubious honor. It made sense when Sam was the owner. They pretty much liked having the chairman of the board running the company because she had more at stake than any of them. They had to know she'd run it for profit."

Jennifer had the uneasy feeling that she should check into the ownership a little more thoroughly. "I know you think it's a dead end, Leo, but is there a file or anything I can see that would give me a little more on the agency?"

"It might be at her office; it might be in her desk in the den upstairs. If the permission is mine to give, you have it. I'm not sure it's all legally mine yet until it goes through litigation, so you might have trouble getting into the files at her office. Check the den; be my guest."

Mark came down with two suitcases and carried them out to the car. "I'd really like to look through her papers, Leo, but I don't want to hold you up."

"Nonsense, you won't hold me up. Just lock up when you're through. The lights are on timers. You might let Mrs.Fritzee know so she doesn't call the cops." He embraced her briefly and gently and thanked her for listening and understanding.

"Just take care of yourself," she said. "I'm not goin' back to work until you do."

Mark winked at her, but she pretended not to notice. After calling Mrs. Fritzee, Jennifer phoned Jim to tell him she would be a little late. "But I still need to talk to you tonight," she said. "Nine o'clock too late?"

"Are you kidding? Anytime, anywhere, kid."

She laughed. "The Pancake House on Western."

"Pretty late breakfast," he said. "See you then."


Jennifer had always been fascinated by personal papers. She would rather nose around in someone's desk than in their closet or even in their safe.

It didn't take her long to determine that Samantha Stanton kept excellent records, and while most of the day-to day business papers were apparently kept at the office, what Jennifer really needed was right there.

In a file labeled "Board," Jennifer found the minutes of the semi-annual meetings of the stockholders of the Gateway Travel Agency. Most were mundane financial reports and guest appearances by various staff members, reporting to the stock holders on different aspects of the company.

Jennifer traced the history of the company from the time Mrs. Stanton bought in and became the major stockholder. The technology and the

relationships with airlines were the most dramatic differences, with Samantha campaigning for total computerization of the operation.

Most interesting, she found that the two most vocal members of the board were Kimberly Rand, the wife half of the Texas couple—Mr. and Mrs. T. J. Rand—and a lawyer named Conrad Dennison, who represented the holding company K.R.C. Limited.

The investment banker, Wilfred Griffin, seemed a positive man from the minutes, always the first to express appreciation ("I'm sure on behalf of the entire board—") for anything and everything presented.

Mr. Rand always backed up his wife, but rarely led any dissent. Dennison was the troublemaker, frequently asking tough, accusatory questions and debating the majority on almost every vote.

On three separate occasions, Dennison tendered cash offers for the stock of both the Rands and Griffin in the middle of a business meeting. On two other occasions, official complaints were noted in the minutes—once by the Rands and once by Samantha Stanton herself—citing the lack of proper procedure in tender offers he had made between meetings.

Chairman: "Let the minutes show that the representative for K.R.C. Ltd. made an improper offer to purchase 60 percent of my stock or 30 percent of the company, tendering his offer by phone and without proper documentation."

K.R.C.: "What's the purpose of putting that in the minutes? I have every right to make a bid for a total majority, and you have every right to refuse it. It appears here as if I've broken some law."

Chairman: "If you need the reminder, our bylaws call for the knowledge of the entire body notified by mail before any such transaction is undertaken. And for the record, my stock is not for sale at any price."

K.R.C.: "We'll see. I just wonder how profitably this company could be run with proper majority control."

Griffin: "I feel very good about how the company is being run. We survived the recession with just one losing quarter, and we've been very profitable for many years."

K.R.C.: "Perhaps our ideas of profits differ, Mr. Griffin. This company is mostly a liability to my clients, almost a tax write-off. It could be twice as profitable."

Jennifer wanted to meet the Conrad Dennison character representing K.R.C. She also wondered who was behind K.R.C. If, by any chance, it was connected with anyone already owning one of the smaller shares, the

purchase of the remaining small share would put half the stock in their hands. Then the real battle would begin.

The addresses and phone numbers were all there, so Jennifer took as many notes as she could and tried to keep it all straight in her head. Just as she was about to put everything back where she found it, she noticed a pile of unopened mail.

Much of it consisted of bills and junk mail addressed to Leo. But a few pieces were for Samantha. Apparently, Leo had dumped everything on her desk that wasn't obviously a sympathy card.

At the bottom of the stack was an unopened six by nine manila envelope from K.R.C. Ltd., addressed to Samantha over her agency title. Leo had said to be his guest. Did that permit her to open his mail? His wife's mail? would she be violating the law—opening a dead woman's mail? The woman's heir had given her permission, sort of.

This was agency business. Leo would be inheriting majority stock. Did that give him total right to this envelope? And if so, had he given Jennifer the right to open it?

It was much too early to call Wisconsin and get Leo's permission. What about the *Day* lawyer who had represented Jennifer a couple of times? No, he would want to know who she was talking about, and he would advise against it.

He would advise against it, she knew, because it was wrong. Maybe Jim would know if there was anyway she could justify it. She dialed. No answer at his apartment. She called his precinct station house. No, he had already left for the day.

Jennifer looked at her watch. It was almost time to leave if she was going to meet Jim at nine o'clock. She held the envelope up to the light. Nothing. Too thick. She studied the outside carefully.

It had been typed in legal typeface, and the name Dennison had been added, also typewritten, above the return address logo. K.R.C. Ltd. had an Evanston post office box, but the office address was on North Sheridan Road in Chicago.

Was it a firm in its own right, or was it simply represented by Conrad Dennison's law firm? How could she know? How could she find out?

Curiosity was killing her. The postmark was the previous week. It must have arrived Friday or Saturday. No earlier, or Mrs. Stanton would have opened it.

What if it was a proper legal offer, a copy of which was mailed to all the other stockholders? Shouldn't Leo be made aware of it? But then, nothing could be transacted until Sanantha's will was executed, right? Leo'd be protected.

But what if an offer was being made on another minority stockholder, and Leo wanted to match or beat the offer? If they didn't hear from Leo by a certain time, the deal would be consummated. Then what?

And what if Jennifer was right about K.R.C. representing someone else on the board? Leo could get back into his daily routine, show up at his first board meeting, and find he was majority stockholder with just forty shares to K.R.C.'s thirty-seven and one half.

All of a sudden the bidding for the remaining two shares—June Roloff's 10 percent and the unsold 12 1/2 percenter—would become fierce. Leo should be aware, shouldn't he? Wasn't it Jennifer's duty to her boss and friend?

She knew it was not.

Twenty minutes later Jennifer was pouring out the story to Jim in the parking lot of the Pancake House. He tried to slow her down and quiet her down as they entered and found a table, but she was going on and on about her dilemma.

He smiled, just listening to her. She sped through the information she had read in the minutes and dwelt on the curious envelope, the one she just didn't think she could resist. It drew her like a magnet.

"I worked like everything to talk myself out of opening it," she said.

He nodded. "Good."

"And then I tried everything to talk myself *into* opening it."

He stopped nodding. "You didn't."

She dug in her bag and produced the envelope. "I hoped it would have one of those gummy flaps that could be pulled apart and then resealed."

"But it didn't?"

"No."

"That's good, because that wouldn't have made it any more right or wrong to do."

"But, Jim, you should see what it says."

His eyes fell. "You didn't."

She held it up to his face. The envelope had been slit. "Just wait till you hear what it's all about."

# Seven

"Just water, please," Jim told the waitress eveniy. "I'm not eating."

"I am!" Jennifer said. "I'm famished. Give me the blueberry pancakes and the works."

"The works?"

"Whatever comes with it-everything. Hash browns, toast, milk, orange juice—whatever."

"Only syrup and whipped cream comes with it, ma'am."

"Fine."

Jim was stony. His eyes appeared hooded, and he sat with his chin in his hand, staring at her, expressionless, as she recounted what she'd found in the envelope. "I'm not sure I want to be party to this," he said at one point.

"You don't have to be," she said. "I know I'm in this alone. But Leo won't mind. Believe me—I know him."

"He may forgive you, Jenn. But it was still wrong to do it without asking first."

"I couldn't reach him! And I couldn't wait. I was right. It's important, and he needs to know about it."

Jim shrugged, and Jennifer sensed frustration building inside her. He was coming off a little pious in this, as if he and the rest of the police didn't go snooping when they felt like it. "You want to hear this or not?" she asked.

He didn't respond, which embarrassed her. So she began without looking at him. "You see, it's notification to all stockholders that KR.C. Ltd. is making an official offer to buy out Mr. Griffin's twelve and a half percent. He's the investment banker with one of the small shares.

"The way it works in this kind of company is that the offer does not have to be matched or even accepted. But if it *is* accepted, or if there is an indication that it will be accepted, other stockholders may tender private bids of their own, without knowing the original bid."

She waited to see if Jim had any questions. He remained in the same posture, staring at her as if disappointed. He *was* disappointed. He had already made that clear.

"So," she concluded, "K.R.C. has notified the seller and the other stockholders of its intention. If the buyer doesn't hear anything by Friday of this week, the offer will be official. Now this Griffin has always been happy with his investment, but with the death of the principal stockholder, he may accept a good price. He's no dummy, and he has not been real active in the decisions of the company. He's just gone along with everything Mrs. Stanton wanted to do."

Jim would not participate in the discussion.

"Don't you think Griffin might want to get out," she pressed, "knowing that Mr. Stanton has no interest in running the business and also knowing that K.R.C. will undoubtedly take over the majority stock eventually?"

No response.

Jennifer ate, occasionally glancing up to see Jim staring at her, still unsmiling. She smiled at him. He looked away. She'd rather he told her off than put her off like this. She lost her appetite quickly.

"OK, all right," she said. "I think you've carried this judgment far enough. I was wrong. I admit it. I'm frankly glad I did it, though, because I think Leo will want to know. All right? Are you going to hate me forever because I didn't live up to your ideal of me?"

Jim just sat looking at her, letting the words echo in her mind so she could hear herself. She only felt worse.

"Do you realize," he said finally, "that you're sidetracked from your mission?"

She looked puzzled.

"Your job is to prove that your boss's wife didn't commit suicide. Based on what was found in her body, it was either suicide or murder. Couldn't have been an accident. How has this mail you've tampered with helped you determine her murderer?"

Jennifer sat back and sighed. She was still upset at Jim's condescending attitude, but she wished she had an answer for that one. All of a sudden she was running the travel agency instead of protecting Samantha Stanton's reputation.

"Jennifer, you have to tell Leo what you've done. You can't let it go long. These things have a way of catching up with us."

Now she was mad. "All right, Jim, I'll call Leo now! Is this thing so serious with you that it harms your view of me?"

"Why put it on me? It was wrong, and we both know it. You're entitled to mistakes; that doesn't shatter me. But I do wish you'd quit trying to justify it and would just deal with it!"

She stomped off to the pay phone, knowing Jim was right, wishing he wasn't, and mad at herself for going against her own conscience. She also wondered what Leo would say.

"He's sleeping, Jennifer," Mark said. "And guess where?"

"Not in the car."

"In the car. And I mean he's out like a light. The weather's nice, and the car's right next to my bedroom window, so I can keep an eye on him. I'm gonna let him sleep. I'm glad you called though. Dad got all worked up when he remembered that some letter was still on the desk from one of the company stockholders."

"That's what I was calling about."

"Good. He called the lawyer at the newspaper and the guy agreed to represent Dad in the agency, help him hire someone to take it over, and all that. He said to just leave that envelope unopened, because if it's any kind of official business, it'll be null and void or something like that as soon as the Lawyer points out that it arrived during the week of my mother's death. OK?"

"That's the problem, Mark. I opened it."

"You opened it? Why would you open it?"

"I thought it might be something important. And it was."

There was silence on the other end for several seconds. "Oh, boy," Mark said finally. "Dad's not going to like that. Neither will his lawyer."

"I was trying to help."

"By opening his mail? I'm not sure how that helps, Jennifer."

"Me either," she muttered.

"Pardon me?"

"Listen, Mark, since what's done is done, you'd better get the message to the lawyer so he can do something about it."

"What's done is done? That's your view of it?"

Jennifer sighed and rolled her eyes. *Not from this guy too!*

"I'm sorry. I shouldn't have. I tried to reach you, but it was too early."

"We tried to reach you just before nine," he said.

"I was gone already. Are you going to chastise me for it, or are you going to tell the lawyer?"

"I'll tell him," he said. "But I think I'll let you tell Dad. You owe me that, at least."

"I owe you?"

"I didn't open his mail."

Jennifer reminded herself that Mark was grieving. Maybe if nothing else came of this, his interest in her would wane. That would almost make it worth it. Problem was, she feared the same was happening to Jim. Maybe

he'd back off if he knew she knew he was right. And if he knew his prediction was right. It had indeed caught up with her.

She trudged back to the table and told Jim. He reached across the table and took her hand. "I was a little rough on you, and I shouldn't have been."

"Of course you should have," she said. "I'm even disappointed in me. I could have helped more by leaving it alone. They would have beaten it by not opening it. Now they have to go on the offensive. And like you said, it's totally off the subject of her death."

'"Totally?"

Jennifer shot him a double take. "What are you saying?"

"Think, Jenn. You didn't get into that desk to look for some partner buying another partner out, did you? Didn't you have a reason you wanted to know more about that business? Wasn't it related to your original purpose here?"

"Yes, I was looking for a murderer."

"Of course. That might sound a little silly now, but you can't leave any stone unturned. It was a hunch, and you played it. What did you expect to find?"

"Some irregularity, some enemy, some reason someone might benefit from Samantha Stanton's death."

"And did you find it?"

"I'm not sure."

"But you've got plenty to go on, lots to check out before you pull out from under this rock, am I right?"

"You're right. When do you become a detective, Sweetheart?"

"Not soon enough."

"Tonight, I think. Thanks. Now aren't you hungry?"

"As a matter of fact, I am. You got time to watch me eat.?"

"Depends. What are you ordering?"

"Just what you did."

"Want what's left of mine?"

"Oh, sure. Cold pancakes are one of my favorites."

The next morning she called Jim before heading out to talk to the two pharmacists on her list. "I saw you angry with me last night."

"For the first time?" he asked.

"You tell me. Have there been other times?"

"I dunno."

"You do too! I can tell from your voice! When?"

"I don't remember."

"You do—"

"No, I really don't. I just know it hasn't been the first time, that's all. Maybe a long time ago. Last night I just decided to let you know it, that's all."

"That one of your philosophies? If it's important enough, you'll tell me, and if it isn't, you'll let it slide?"

"I guess."

"Is that good?" she asked.

"I think so."

"So do I. Any more thoughts before I go out and play detective today, Sergeant Purcell?"

"Uh, what are you expecting from the pharmacists today, Jenn? They're a pretty tightlipped bunch unless you have a warrant or something."

"I know. But apparently there was nothing wrong with the two isolated ingredients she might have gotten at different times."

"Still, they're prescription drugs, so there would have to be a record."

"Of course, my theory is that there will be no record whatever of her purchasing the ingredients."

"I thought of another obstacle you should be aware of. Maybe you already know."

"Go ahead. I need whatever I can get."

"It's just that Mrs. Stanton's philosophy and politics are not in your favor. The minister, or whatever he was, did a good job avoiding the suicide angle at the funeral, but the fact is, she might have been comfortable discussing just those ways to die. Not that she would have. Nothing in her history or personality indicates that she would have chosen it for herself, but can't you see her arguing for euthanasia under the right circumstances?"

"I guess, but unless she had some terminal illness, which the coroner didn't find—either that, or Jake's not saying—she certainly wouldn't have been preoccupied with it from the perspective of her own life."

"I agree. Just something to think about."

"Anything else?" she said.

"Yeah, matter of fact. Just before we left last night, you recounted Mrs. Stanton's morning regimen. Did you come to any conclusions based on that?"

Jennifer thought a moment. "Well, yeah," she said. "I guess I just thought they were kind of obvious."

"Don't ever assume that."

"Well, I thought they all pointed to the fact that she was on her way to work, not on her way to commit suicide."

"I agree," he said, "but tell me why."

"Dressed. Made up. Had her tea. Did the dishes. Brought the paper in. Had brushed her teeth, rinsed with mouth wash, and put lipstick on."

"You know that for sure?"

"I know about the lipstick from Jake Steinmetz. I'm guessing on the teeth brushing or mouth wash."

"Jake could tell you that. Better find out."

"Important?"

"Sure. Any change at all in her morning routine could blow your theory. Anything at all that even hints that her mind was elsewhere. So far, everything rings true. She was in a pattern, a habit, nothing changed. That's not how suicides work. They might get gussied up or do a few habitual things, but not everything. What would be the point? And what would it say about her state of mind?"

"Jim, I'm saying the woman was doing what she always did. She was on her way to work."

"Why did she take a pill, Jennifer? If someone forced her, they had to have been there. And if they were there, someone would have seen them. And they would have had to have known her habits, her schedule, when she did what. Any evidence of that?"

Jennifer thought. "No. I'll ask around, but up to now, no. Nothing like that. You know my theory on that?"

"Hm."

"That pill was in her aspirin bottle, and it was a time bomb. Someone planted it—who knows how long ago and waited for her to get to it."

"Would Leo remember if she had a headache the night before? Or that morning?"

"I'll check. Why?"

"Maybe it wasn't even a bottle she always carried with her. Maybe it was a common bottle they had in the cabinet in the bathroom. If she had a headache, she might have grabbed a tablet and tossed the bottle in her purse for the work day."

"Could be. And if so, what are you thinking?"

"You sure they didn't plant it in the bottle when the bottle was in the cabinet?"

"Jim! It sounds like you're still thinking it could have been Leo!"

"Not at all. What I'm suggesting is that the intended *victim* could have been Leo."

# Eight

Jennifer knew she'd hit some sort of pay dirt the minute she walked into the Hargreaves Drugstore on Western Avenue a few blocks from Leo's house. It was as if she was expected.

As soon as she mentioned wanting to ask some questions, she saw movement in the back, and by the time she mentioned her name, her newspaper, and the name Stanton, someone was gone out the door, and the ledger book was pulled off the counter.

Angry and full of adrenalin, Jennifer spotted a service entrance and dashed outside just in time to see an older man getting into a late model Oldsmobile, a raincoat over his white smock.

She ran up to the car door before he could shut it and leaned in, daring him to slam it on her. "You must be Mr. Hargreaves," she said sweetly.

"That's right," he said, shoulders slumping, hands in his lap.

"Apparently you know what I want to talk to you about."

He nodded miserably. "Do you know this could ruin a family business that's been in this neighborhood more'n fifty years?"

"What could?"

"What you want to talk to me about."

"What do I want to talk to you about.?"

"You tell me."

"Let's quit playing games, Mr. Hargreaves. You've as much as admitted that your pharmacy made available drugs that killed someone. Why not just tell me about it?"

"For the paper? I don't have to talk, you know."

"Off-the-record. For my peace of mind. And the husband's peace of mind. For your peace of mind too, I imagine."

That struck a chord with the old man. "Take a ride with me," he said. She ran around and jumped in the other side.

He drove about six blocks to a muddy public park where baby-sitters watched day care center kids playing on the swings and bars. He turned off the engine and swung his right knee up onto the seat beside him.

Jennifer guessed him at about retirement age. He was dark complexioned and had long, wavy, salt-and-pepper hair. His accent had a faint British clip to it. He sounded weary.

"I ran errands for my father in the twenties in that store," he said.

She nodded.

"I'd hate to see anything happen to it. If you'll tell me again you're not going to print this in the paper, maybe I can tell you something that will help everybody concerned."

She nodded again.

"Well," he said with a sigh, "we have rules. We're pretty strict. Have to be. State agencies are tougher on us all the time with all the dope problems and everything. The people who work for me are either family or they're carefully trained. I mean, the family is trained too, you understand, but they're making a career of it. Everyone has to take all the classes, pass all the tests, get all the apprentice licenses and all that."

"I see."

"What I'm getting at is this. Yes, sometimes we make an exception, do somebody a favor. But there are a lot of prerequisites, if you know what I mean."

"Tell me."

"For instance, I might fill a prescription two or even three times past what the physician has indicated on the slip. But, nobody else in the shop can do it. They have to call me. And first, I have to know the customer."

"And the doctor?"

"That goes without saying. I would never, ever fill a prescription from a doctor who didn't have references, a local address, all that, at least with your dangerous drugs."

"OK."

"So, I'm at home, all right? I get a call early one evening from one of my nephews. A good kid. A little young, but a lot of promise. Goes by the book. I like him. He'll make it. He asks me if he can give Mrs. Stanton a few grams of something. It was nothing, but it was a puzzle because she had called it in first. Said she had had to get it somewhere else last time for some reason—which puzzled me because she trades with us all the time, and we're usually open.

"But anyway, she's told my nephew that she needed a little more and that she would read it to him from off the prescription slip. He'd asked her if there was a filling limit. She'd said no. Now normally, he could have filled that because she would then bring the slip in, and he would match it with the dosage and everything would be kosher.

"But the reason he calls me is that she's done all this, but when she gets there, she's forgotten the slip. She says she'll bring it in sometime, and he knows I'll have his hide if he doesn't check with me."

"So what did you do?"

"Without a second thought, I thanked him, praised him for calling me, told him 'no problem, it's always smart to call.'"

"And?"

"And I tell him to give her the prescription and don't make a big deal about bringing the prescription in. We don't want to treat her like we don't trust her, a longtime customer like that."

"When did you realize you'd given her something that would prove lethal?"

"Not till I heard about her suicide. I'm tellin' you, I cried. I was scared. I still am. I'm kickin' myself. Not that I could have stopped her. A woman wants to kill herself, she's going to do it with or without my help, you understand. But if I'd been firm, not made exceptions for an old customer and a respected doctor, who knows? Maybe I could have slowed her down, made her think twice. You know."

"Did you check with her doctor?"

"Billings? I was afraid to. What if he says, 'No, I never prescribed that'— which he probably didn't, because by itself it's virtually worthless. Then he would find out I filled a bogus prescription, and there goes my credibility with him, let alone everyone else."

"Aren't you curious to know where she got the other ingredient?"

"Sure. I assumed it would be from the drugstore up here on Kedzie, being so close, but again, I wasn't about to call and ask."

"Did Mrs. Stanton pay by check or put it on her bill?"

"Neither. She paid cash. That was a little unusual, come to think of it, because she has an active account with us. Her husband usually picks up the medicine though. But it was a small amount, so I didn't think anything of it."

Jennifer was crushed, and it showed.

"I'm sorry," he said. "I feel terrible about it too."

"It's not that Mr. Hargreaves. I appreciate your telling me, and I understand why you'd be scared. It's just that up to this moment, I didn't believe Mrs. Stanton committed suicide."

He nodded slightly, understanding. "And now you have to tell her husband?"

"Eventually."

"I wish there was a way you could tell him that we did it in good faith, if you have to tell him."

"I believe you did it in good faith. There's no doubt it was her, was there, sir?"

"Not really, no. It's kind of embarrassing, but I always thought Mrs. Stanton was a pretty nice looking woman. Didn't you? Did you know her?"

"Yes. Yes I did, and yes she was."

"Well, I asked my nephew when he had her standin' right there in the store, I says, "Is she a good-lookin' redhead?' and he kinda whispered into the phone, 'That's her, Unc.' "

Jennifer used an entirely different strategy at the Allen Drugs chain store adjacent to the big grocery on Kedzie. Knowing it was a huge place that used a lot of employees, she just marched up to the counter and asked to see the head pharmacist.

"He's off until tomorrow, ma'am."

"Then I'd like to talk to someone who has the authority to let me look through your prescription records for the last two months. I'm from the *Day* and I'm exercising my right based on the Freedom of Information Act."

The young man looked concerned but huddled with an associate pharmacist for a few seconds. The associate approached. "How may I help you?" he asked.

"Exactly the way he told you," she said firmly.

"May I see some identification?" he asked.

Jennifer pointed to the front page of the *Day* which was in a stand near the counter. He looked at the picture of her on the front page, along with the note that she was on assignment. He smiled. "You're prettier in person," he said.

She didn't respond, which seemed to upset him. "I still need to see some identification," he said coldly. She showed him her press card and driver's license. He studied them briefly and pushed them back to her, and as she replaced them in her wallet, he slid the big book around toward her so she could see it.

He said, "You know that the Freedom of Information Act doesn't give you the right to print any of those actual names without permission."

"Journalism one-oh-one," she said, and immediately felt that had been too cold. She added a wink and a smile. He blushed and walked away.

Within seconds, Jennifer located the notation for the small amount of the ingredient needed to make a lethal dose. The date matched the one from Hargreaves, and the doctor was listed as Billings. "An appropriate name for a doctor," Leo had once deadpanned, but now it didn't seem so funny.

Next to the listing, however, was a notation. *No prescription. Verified with phys. by phone. Pd. cash.*

Dr. Floyd Billings was a stocky, pleasant, soft-spoken man who agreed to meet with Jennifer at the end of his office hours, about six-thirty. He loosened his smock and sat across the desk from her in a small examining room.

"I was as shocked as anyone when Mrs. Stanton took her own life," he said. "I knew she had not told her husband of her problem, but I assume she left him a note."

"There was no note, doctor. That's why we've been convinced it was not a suicide. What was her problem?"

"Oh, I'm afraid I would not be at liberty to say, even though she's dead. That is very privileged information. She made me pledge not to tell her husband, a pledge I would now break. But you understand that I couldn't tell you."

"But you would tell Leo?"

"I would."

"I understand. Could you at least tell me if her problem was terminal?"

"I really shouldn't discuss it. I'm sorry."

"Dr. Billings, do you recall receiving a phone call—it would have been two months ago to the day yesterday from Allen Drugs?"

"Well, I get so many."

"Mrs. Stanton was there without a prescription, but they called you to verify that it was all right to give her the medicine."

He furrowed his brow. "I *do* recall something like that. Yes! I remember."

"Do you recall what the medicine was?"

"I didn't ask."

"Excuse me?"

"I didn't ask. I had my girl look up her charts real quick and tell me if we had prescribed anything out of the ordinary lately. She said no, so I told the druggist to refill whatever she was asking for."

"Would you like to see what she asked for?"

He nodded and leaned forward to take the small slip of paper from Jennifer. Reading it, he winced and paled. He carefully laid the paper on the desk in front of him and ran his fingers over his face.

"She was a patient of mine for decades," he said, his voice weak. "I mean it. At least three decades. She must have had a breakdown of some sort. She must have."

"You've said you were shocked when you heard of her death, and you can't believe she would do something like this after you had known her

for so long, so I'm guessing that whatever physical problem she might have had was not terminal. Otherwise this might have all made some sense to you. Am I right?"

"I'd rather not discuss it. Are you going to report me for this lack of discretion? In retrospect, of course, I can see what a terrible mistake I made. Those precautions we're supposed to use are to protect us from drug addicts, not our own patients."

"I don't think anything would be served by my telling anyone. When you tell Mr. Stanton about his wife's problem, you might want to tell him these details."

"Perhaps you're right. I don't look forward to that."

"You"ll have some time," she said.

Jennifer didn't look forward to talking to Leo again herself.

# Nine

The next morning, Jennifer phoned Leo's Wisconsin cottage. As expected, Mark answered.

"Is Leo mad?" Jennifer asked.

"Well, I don't think he cares to speak to you, if that's what you mean."

"Are you serious?"

Mark didn't respond, and Jennifer was worried.

"Mark, I need to know if your mother was ill, either in the night before she died or that morning. Was there a headache or any other sort of ailment? Can you find out from your father and let me know? I want to know why she took an aspirin."

Mark was still silent.

"Mark?" she said tentatively.

"Hm."

"Are you there?"

"I miss you," he said, flatly.

She pursed her lips. She was thinking, *Oh, for pete's sake, grow up. You're acting like a child! I'm engaged, I'm busy, and I don't have time for fun and games right now.* But she didn't respond. She decided she could play the game the same way he did. She figured there was nothing quite as frustrating as being ignored by phone.

She pretended Mark hadn't said anything. "Can you find out for me?" she repeated.

"I know how you feel about me," he said, desperately.

*That's a laugh,* she thought, pitying him.

"And you'll either call me or have your father call me, OK?"

"Bye-bye," Mark said endearingly.

Jennifer nearly gagged. This was all she needed in the middle of a frustrating and disappointing investigation. She was trying to muster the courage she would need to tell Leo the bad news—that his wife had indeed apparently stretched the truth to the breaking point to get the combination of contraband drugs that killed her.

Jennifer spent the rest of the morning studying her notes, wondering where to turn and what to look for that might make the evidence look less certain. She and Jim would be going to prayer meeting at their church that night. She had already requested prayer for her boss, whose wife had died. But how could she ask for prayer that it was other than a suicide?

She finally decided to console herself by making an appointment to talk with someone who would likely agree with her—someone who would feel too that, in spite of all the evidence, Samantha Stanton could not have taken her own life. She called Mrs. Stanton's best friend.

June Roloff invited her to lunch. "As long as you don't put yourself out," Jennifer said.

"Nonsense," she said in a pleasantly low voice.

"I could just as easily pick you up and take you out somewhere," Jennifer suggested.

"Really, it'll be no problem," Mrs. Roloff said.

Jennifer had met the striking fifty-year-old brunette before, but she had not realized what a swank neighborhood the Roloffs lived in, or even that they had domestic help. Their exquisite lunch of light crepes and fresh fruit was served as they sat on a wrought iron and glass sun deck.

Jennifer wanted to blurt out the question: Where in their world did the Roloffs get the money for a place like that? But she just tried to take it in stride. It was apparent that Mrs. Roloff was still grieving. Her eyes filled with tears whenever she reminisced about Samantha.

"I'm being asked to teach her class and even to lead some of her travel tours now," she said. "I just don't know if I can, or if I should."

"Why not?" Jennifer asked. "It would be for her, wouldn't it?"

"I suppose, maybe. Yes, it might. But it would be so painful, so difficult. I'm not another Samantha, and I don't want to pretend to be."

The woman spent much of the afternoon talking about her many adventures with Samantha. "We traveled quite a bit together, you know."

Jennifer nodded.

"She left a little piece of Gateway to me," June said. "I was so touched, I cried and cried. It was so sweet of her."

"When did you find out?" Jennifer asked. "I was under the impression that the will had not been executed yet."

"Oh, it hasn't, but Samantha told me she was going to do that about six months ago. She even showed me a copy of the will."

"You must have been very moved."

"It was unlike any feeling in the world. That agency had become her life, outside of Leo, of course. She couldn't have left me anything more personal unless she had left me her family."

And she clouded over again.

"Mrs. Roloff, I know you're upset, but I want to confide in you, and I have to admit, the news is not good. May I?"

"I guess."

"I've been researching this death under the assumption that Samantha Stanton would be the last person in the world to commit suicide. I admit I was biased. I was looking for the evidence I wanted to find. Much of it is puzzling, but the majority is troubling."

"In what way?"

"In that it is becoming apparent that Mrs. Stanton may have indeed taken her own life."

"And that surprises you?" Mrs. Roloff asked.

"Your response surprises me," Jennifer said.

"Why?"

"Well, I, because I just assumed, I mean—I didn't think you thought it was suicide." "Why not?"

"Because you knew her. Leo lived with her, and he's convinced it wasn't suicide."

"If it wasn't suicide, what was it?" Mrs. Roloff said. "An accident?"

"I was thinking more in terms—"

"Because if it wasn't an accident or suicide, it was murder, and one thing I'm certain of, Sam didn't have any enemies—at least not any who would have murdered her."

"Who were her enemies?"

"I wouldn't even know that. I know she had some run-ins with certain stockholders in her company, but nothing serious. She always speculated that one of the representatives of one of the owners was in cahoots with some old couple on the board, but I never got any of the specifics, and it certainly didn't sound like she had developed any serious conflicts."

"Then you think it was an accident, Mrs. Roloff?"

June Roloff stood and stared out through the glass at her withering garden. "You mistake grief and loss for naiveté," she said. "You forget that we were like sisters."

Jennifer was shocked. "Are you telling me you think she committed suicide?"

"I try not to think about it," she said.

"But were you close enough to know what Dr. Billings knew?"

"Of course. I always thought she should have told Leo. It wasn't going to kill her. The sugar in her blood would eventually affect her eyesight. It already had, of course. But she was a lot of years from hardening of the arteries. She had a lot of good years left. Maybe as many as twenty."

"Why do you think she didn't tell Leo?"

"I think she thought it would make her less of a woman. She was within a year of having to give herself insulin injections. I don't think she was quite ready for that."

"I still don't see her killing herself."

"It's hard for me too," Mrs. Roloff said. "Though not totally surprising."

"Why haven't you told Leo?"

"I didn't know if he really didn't believe it, or if he simply wasn't accepting it. He will eventually. He needs his illusions right now."

"Then I'm wild-goose chasing."

"Jennifer, there is nothing that would please me more than for you to discover that I'm wrong. It horrifies me to think that she's gone, and to add the nightmare that she is gone by her own hand when Leo and I and so many loved her so deeply. I just don't want to accept that either. But it happened, and I'm trying to cope. Keep searching until you're satisfied."

"But you're implying that I am not going to like what I find."

"You haven't so far."

"For the most part, no."

"For the most part?"

"Well, there was shoddy police work that could have messed things up. There was the fact that Samantha wasn't despondent, that Leo or anyone knew of anyway." Jennifer's listener betrayed a sad, knowing smile. "And she was all ready for work when she died. Why?"

"Probably because she didn't want anyone to notice," June said. "She wasn't the type to do anything for show. She wouldn't have faked an attempt just to get Leo's attention. She did it so it would be discovered after it was done. That's my guess."

"That must be very difficult for you to even think about."

"Right."

"Is there more?" Jennifer asked.

"More?"

"More reason to believe it was suicide and not an accident or murder."

"Well, a person doesn't accidentally kill herself with a dose like that one. That rules out accidents, unless it was intended for Leo, and everyone knows that's ludicrous."

Jennifer nodded. "But couldn't it still have been murder?"

"That's almost as painful to consider as suicide."

"But we have to consider it, Mrs. Roloff. Because if it was murder and everyone thinks it's suicide, that means there's a murderer around somewhere. Someone who knew an awful lot about Samantha Stanton's habits."

"Don't go implicating Leo now," Mrs. Roloff said.

"I wouldn't think of it," Jennifer said. "Never."

They sat in silence for several minutes.

"Anything else that will help me?" Jennifer asked finally.

"Nothing you'll be happy about," she said.

"I'll be happy for anything that will bring an end to this assignment I once so eagerly wanted."

"Even if it ends the way you don't want it to?"

"I'm afraid so now. I just have to know, one way or the other."

"You'll need to keep this confidential."

"Of course."

"From everyone."

"Everyone?"

"Absolutely."

"Let me think about that for a moment." Jennifer had the feeling that Samantha's best friend in the world could shed some light on the truth, that she might say something that would be difficult to take, but that there was something to the cliché that the truth hurts. "All right," she said, "I'll keep your confidence."

"How do you think Samantha got those euthanasia booklets?"

Jennifer blinked. "I've been hoping to prove that they were planted by a murderer."

"In a way, I wish you were right. Like I said, knowing she was murdered is not any more pleasant than knowing she killed herself, but somehow I feel so guilty about her suicide."

Jennifer wanted to hear where June Roloff thought Samantha had gotten the suicide manuals, but she couldn't let that comment go. *"You* feel guilty about it?"

"Certainly. I was her best friend. Her confidante. I was committed to her. I had responsibilities and obligations to her." She began to cry. "And she did to me too!"

"Such as?"

"She had a commitment, a responsibility to stay alive. I resent that she's gone! I need her! I loved her and cared about her and gave of myself for her. And she did to me too, until this. Leaving without so much as a note or a good-bye—I can hardly bear it."

"But she left you that most personal gift."

"That was a gesture that came long before she died. It was sweet and thoughtful, but I didn't want it this way."

"But why should you feel guilty?"

"Because I was inadequate. I wasn't what she needed. I wasn't enough! She had such deep needs and causes, and I was not up to the challenge.

Because she couldn't find answers anywhere—not even in me—she left us all."

Mrs. Roloff hid her eyes with her hand, but Jennifer had to ask. "Do you know where she got the booklets?"

The older woman nodded, her tear-streaked face finally showing its age. "She dragged me out to one secret meeting of the SMS. You know, Sam and I agreed a lot philosophically, but we parted there."

"The SMS?"

"Simplified Method Society."

"Method of what?"

"Self-euthanasia. Assisted-euthanasia. Call it whatever you like. They advocate suicide as a humane method of death for the terminally ill, or really for anyone who chose it and didn't want it to be painful or messy."

"You actually went with her?"

"She bugged me for ages to go. Asked me to think about it. To consider it. She hit me with dozens of hypothetical situations. What if this and what if that? Some of them were hard to argue with. I suppose there would be situations where I would rather be put out of my misery, even by a friend or relative than to suffer on for years."

"Where does a group like that meet?"

"In local hotels or restaurants. When you come in, they ask if you know what they meet to talk about and to promote. If you say no, they tell you you're not welcome. If you say yes, they ask you to state it briefly. If you're right, you may come in."

"What's the purpose of all that?"

"To make sure no one gets in the wrong room, is then shocked and tells someone who won't understand what it's all about."

"And they distribute this literature?"

"Free. But not to me. No, ma'am. I even used a phony name when I attended. I got the impression most people did. Not Sam though. Nobody could make Sam pretend she was someone else. So there was ol' Samantha Stanton, visiting the euthanasia meeting with her frumpy friend Claudia Brown."

"Frumpy?"

"I even disguised myself, Jennifer! New name and new look. It was creepy, and I never went back." She began to become emotional again. "You see why I can't be terribly surprised at her death—at least her method?"

# Ten

"I agree it looks bleak," Jim said after prayer meeting that night as he and Jennifer strolled a Lake Michigan beach. Strolled might not be the word for it. She huddled against him and hid her face and neck from the chilling wind—happy to be with him, but regretting the choice of the beach.

Finally they sought shelter behind a gigantic tree trunk about sixty feet from the water's edge and settled in the sand with their backs against the wood. Out of the wind and nestled against Jim's chest, Jennifer felt relaxed and secure in the silence.

She had told him the story of her day while they rode to and from the church. "These people seem so empty," she said. "Leo and his son and even Samantha. Mrs. Fritzee. Mrs. Roloff. It's depressing."

"Seems it would give you a chance to talk to them about God," he said.

"You'd think so, and I know this sounds like an excuse, but I start listening to them and empathizing with them, and I get emotional and can't bring myself to tell them of the most important things. I'm overwhelmed with how they're looking in the wrong place for their peace and their answers, but so much so that it's as if I'm incapacitated."

He nodded in sympathy. "What are you thinking now about Samantha's death?"

She shook her head. "I don't know anymore. I just don't know."

"That's a good sign," he said. "Good or bad, depending upon how you look at it."

"What do you mean?"

"I mean it's apparent you haven't made up your mind yet, even though you have evidence heavily weighted one way. That's healthy skepticism in my book; it might be delusion to some people. That's why it's good or bad, depending—"

"My guess is I'm deluding myself, Jim." He didn't respond. It was *her* theory, not his. She continued. "The only reason I think it could still be murder is that her morning routine didn't change one iota and because I knew the woman."

"You *thought* you knew the woman," he said.

She nodded. "Leo thought he knew the woman too."

"I would agree with Leo."

"But Jim, Leo says she didn't commit suicide."

"I'd say he knows better than anyone."

"You agree with him?"

"That's what I said."

"I do too."

"I know you do, Jenn."

"How did you know?"

"Besides the fact that it's written all over you?"

"Uh-huh."

"Because you're staring at two drugstores, a doctor, a best friend, a coroner, the cops, and the evidence, and they all say it was suicide. Yet you're undecided. To me, that's not undecided. To me, you're coming down on the side of murder."

"But why am I, Jim? Am I that smart—or that stupid?"

"I'd like to think your intuition is good. It could be blind loyalty to your boss."

"Which he could also be guilty of Jim: blind loyalty to his wife."

"Right. But I am sure of this, the truth will surface. It always does."

"Always?"

"As long as people keep looking for it."

"How long will I have to look?"

"That's entirely up to you."

"And up to my bosses," she said. Jim chuckled. "I'm not sure I know where to turn next."

"That's a detective's greatest position," he said. "When you don't know where to turn next, turn everywhere. Get general. Stop being so specific. Think of all the places and people you've heard about so far, what you've learned, what questions have been raised. Anything you're thinking or wondering about?"

"Yeah," she said. "I'd like to meet some of the people behind Gateway Travel. I'd like to check in again with the coroner to find out about toothpaste or mouth wash in Mrs. Stanton's body. I want to hear back from Casanova about whether his father remembers if his mother had a headache sometime just before her death."

"Go for all of 'em, Jenn, but don't leave out an important one."

"I'm listening."

"Hadn't you better attend an SMS meeting?"

"In disguise, of course."

"Of course."

Coroner Jacob Steinmetz, M.D., stared at Jennifer from over the tops of his halfglasses the next morning in his office. "I said nothing about sugar content in the blood," he said, "and I dare say her personal physician didn't either."

Jennifer just returned his gaze.

"We noted something about the eye muscle and tissue," he said. "That's all, if your sugar guess is based on the transcript of the autopsy. You can't necessarily assume diabetes based on glaucoma."

"Any evidence she was a marijuana user?"

"That would be extremely difficult to determine by autopsy unless she had inhaled the smoke shortly before death. We didn't find any such trace. Why?"

"Isn't it common for glaucoma sufferers to even be *prescribed* marijuana?"

"Not common. Bandied about in sensational journals, I suppose. But no, not common in this country. Don't impugn a fine doctor like Billings. He's a good man."

"Tell me about the residue on her teeth or gums."

"Standard. Food particles. Tooth paste. Mouth wash."

"Alcohol?"

"Only from the mouth wash."

"How do you know that?"

"From the amount. C'mon, Jennifer, you're fishing. Let's get on with this so I can get back to work, huh? I wish *you* would too. I like you better when you're interviewing me for a story, not as an amateur detective."

"That hurt," she said, seriously. He didn't respond. She quickly recovered and plunged ahead. "I want to know," she said, "if you could tell whether Mrs. Stanton had a headache within twelve hours of her death or whether the poison would have obliterated such evidence."

"No, the poison would not have duplicated the blood vessel trauma created by a headache. However, death sometimes releases the pressure on the brain, and the headache symptoms go away."

"Was that the case in her death?"

"Why are you curious about a headache, Jennifer?"

"Well, I don't know, but apparently my hunch was right, because you're already evading the question."

"I won't evade it if you'll tell me where you're going with this."

"You've got a deal. You first."

"The woman was suffering from a severe headache, just short of a migraine, possibly up to six hours before her death. There's evidence she took some aspirin in the middle of the night."

"I don't recall that from our first conversation, Jake."

"We didn't have a deal then, Jennifer."

"Must I always make a deal to get straight answers?"

"Always," he said, smiling. "Now what're you making of all this?"

"The woman was murdered, Jake. Someone slipped a bogus pill into her aspirin bottle. If she wanted to kill herself, why not in the middle of the night while her head was throbbing?"

"Maybe she didn't want her husband to wake up next to her corpse."

"And maybe I'm right," she said.

"So you're saying someone slipped the pill into her bottle, possibly a long time before her death. Because they couldn't know when she was going to have a headache."

"I guess."

"Unless they poisoned her just a little the day before to make her feel the need of an aspirin." He was teasing her, and she resented it. "And how were they to know that she wouldn't share the bottle with her husband and wind up killing him unintentionally? Really, Jennifer, you're barking up the wrong—"

"The woman was dressed for work, Jake, and she completed her morning regimen right through to the tooth brushing and the mouth wash."

"And if the murderer planted the suicide pill, how did he know when to plant the euthanasia booklets so it would look like a suicide?"

Jennifer didn't know what to say. A murderer would have had no way of knowing when Mrs. Stanton would take the fatal pill, so how could the books have been planted?

Jennifer stood. "I'm going to prove Samantha Stanton didn't kill herself, Jake. But it won't be out of any malice toward you. Can we still be friends, no matter how it turns out?"

He smiled weakly. "Sure. Just promise me you won't have the body exhumed. I hate disinterred bodies. Messy all the way around. Families don't like it. Nobody does."

"I promise to avoid that if possible," she said, knowing Leo would probably oppose it too. That is, unless he felt it was absolutely necessary to clear his wife's name.

Mr. T. J. Rand—even by telephone from Texas was not at all what Jennifer expected. She thought he'd be a big-talking loudmouth with a

twangy drawl. The drawl was there all right, but with no twang, no volume, and no bragging.

"I don't rightly know why Mr. Dennison is makin' a bid now for Mr. Griffin's share. But I cain't hardly blame the man for sellin', now that the principal owner has died and we'll be lookin' frantically for a new working manager, understand?"

"Will you be selling too?"

"Oh my, no!" came the shrill voice of Kimberly Rand, whom Jennifer had not known was even on the line. "Things may never be better! We're still happy with our investment, and frankly, I can get excited about Mr. Dennison's clients taking a little more control in the company."

Jennifer decided to go on the offensive. "There are those who suspect that Mr. Dennison actually represents some other stockholder and that the purchase will then represent an even larger portion of the company."

"I have to get off now, T. J.," Kimberly said. "I got no more time for speculation with someone I don't even know. You get off the phone soon too, you hear?"

"Yes, dear. Well, Miz Grey, I never really thought o' that. But if the company that Mr. Dennison represents is actually a front for one of the other smaller stockholders, it could only be us. If it was Griffin, he'd be buyin' himself out. Dennison's K.R.C. Limited owns two small shares, so that leaves only us to be the sneaky partner. Is that what you're implyin'?"

"Yes, sir."

"Well, I resent that. First of all, you shoulda just come out an' said it. Second of all, I don't know how you get K.R.C. out of T. J. Rand. Good day, Miz Grey."

Jennifer's appointment with the seller, Wilfred Griffin, was for the mid-afternoon. She found him in his suburban Niles office, which also housed several similar firms. Griffin was one member of a five-principal company that invested mainly in municipal bonds.

"But this deal," he said brightly, with a big smile she assumed was normal, "is strictly independent, strictly personal. I'm rather proud of it. On my own, even when I was a junior member of this firm and didn't have my name on the stationery, I tried to get them to invest in Gateway Travel. It was voted down twice out of hand, and then I was allowed to pitch for it officially, I mean with the whole dog and pony show, you know what I mean?" He didn't wait for a response.

"I mean I had Mrs. Stanton in here, and I had flip charts and slides and earning curves and flowcharts and graphs. I'm tellin' ya, if I'd been an investor, I'd have jumped at it."

"But they didn't?"

"No, they didn't. But did I rub it in when I invested on my own and made a nice piece of change? No, ma'am. Not my style. I didn't even brag about it. But I did make it clear I had taken a chance on my own, just so I could kinda live and die by that one risk—'course, I was convinced it was safe and in fact had great potential—"

"I gathered that."

"Huh? Ha! Yeah! I guess you would. Any—how, I never bragged about quarterly or annual earnings unless someone asked. But when they asked, as they always did—independent of each other and always claiming that if it had been solely up to them, they would have voted for it—I was ready with a little printout to show just how successful and profitable it had been for me. They're all a bunch of liars, of course, because the vote was unanimous against it every time. I mean *every* time. But I don't mind. Those are the kinds of lies I tell too. None of us are actually dishonest; in fact, our firm is honest to a fault. Never cheated a client. Never will. But fudge a little on your own reputation, well—you know what I mean. That's why I was always ready with the printout, because no one would have believed me otherwise.

"Why, would you believe that each *and* every one of them at one time or another has asked how they can buy into the company and whether they can buy *me* out! Would you believe that?"

"Every *one* of them?"

"Every one."

"No, I wouldn't believe that."

"Well, you catch on fast, sweetie, 'cause you're right. Only three of the four have asked to buy me out, but they've all asked the other questions. Believe me?"

"Never again," she said laughing. "I'll never trust another investment banker as long as I live."

He laughed too. "Now, what can I do for you? You're probably wonderin' why in the world this idiot is selling out. I'll tell you straight. I got an offer I couldn't refuse. I got an offer twice what the stock is worth. It's such a good offer that I'm not even worried—and I know the buyer isn't worried in the least—that the other owners will even come close to it. 'Course they won't know what it is, so they'll be at a disadvantage. But I'll bet no one comes within fifty percent of it when they try to *beat* it."

"So, strictly a money deal."

"Exactly."

# Eleven

Jennifer's hope that there was something to chew on in the relationship between Wilfred ("Call me Freddie") Griffin and Samantha Stanton was short-lived.

"I just admired the woman, that's all. Met her husband once. Whale of a nice guy, and talented newspaperman, I understand. But this woman ran that agency like a pro from the day she bought in and became the manager. She'd been there before, you know, but after she came up through the ranks to assistant manager, she had to scrape up some money somewhere and buy in to become manager."

"Was there a problem with the previous manager?" Jennifer asked.

"None, except that the board disliked him. I wasn't there then; this is all hearsay. 'Course, K.R.C. never liked anything or anybody in management, so when I came I tried to balance 'em out a little. Never worked.

"They were right in that case, though, and when Mrs. Stanton bought in and took over, profits went up right away. Wasn't long, though, before Conrad Dennison became the representative for the holding company, and he was pickier than the last guy."

"Do you happen to know where Mrs. Stanton got her money?"

Griffin smiled. "Sure. She told us plenty of times. It was one-third inheritance, one third saved up, and one-third borrowed, long since paid off. Remarkable woman."

"Truly. Do you think there was trouble between Mrs. Stanton and the previous manager?"

"Nah. Just the usual frustrations of workin' for somebody who doesn't do as good a job as you could do. We all deal with that, don't we? Ha!"

"But there's no lingering problem that you know of?"

"Oh, no. I don't even remember the guy's name, but he became a ticket counter man at one of the big airlines at O'Hare. Died about three years ago. Heart attack, I think. I got his name in the file if you want it."

Jennifer shook her head. "Do you think Mrs. Stanton had any enemies on the board?"

Griffin's smile faded and he squinted at her. You mean real enemies? Like murderin' enemies? No. None. We had our squabbles, but no, not at all. Not even Dennison, and he was her biggest critic."

"We'll see," Jennifer said. "Now, Mr. Griffin, I've looked over several sets of minutes of your meetings over the past few years, and I have to ask you why you finally relented and will sell to Dennison. I know the money was good, but aren't you worried about the character of the company?"

"Not really. I know what you're thinking, and I know I've been less than cordial in disagreeing with Mr. Dennison a lot in the meetings, but my share won't give K.R.C. Limited enough power to do anything. Unless he thinks he can buy out the Stanton heir, he's not really helped himself except financially. And despite how much he paid me, if they can find the right manager, he'll have his money inside a decade."

"A decade? Isn't that a long wait?"

"Not for that kind of dough. 'Course, K.R.C. couldn't have known that Mrs. Stanton was going to die, but I'm not going to let him out of the offer. He may try to pull some legal shenanigan now, but I've got him by the short hairs. I was going to turn him down, you know, even at the price he settled at."

"You were?"

"Course I was!"

"What changed your mind?"

"What else? Mrs. Stanton's death."

"You wouldn't have sold even for a big price with her running the show?"

"Nope. Said that many times. I think Mr. Dennison has bought himself a pig in a poke now, but that's his problem."

"Do you think Mrs. Stanton committed suicide?"

"Well, yeah! 'Course! I didn't know that was even a question. I didn't really know the woman enough to know what was troubling her. She certainly couldn't have had money problems unless she was way overextended. But we'd have known if the agency wasn't in tip-top shape, and it always was. I don't know why she killed herself."

"You can't consider the possibility that it was not a suicide?"

"Hm, I don't know. I guess not after seein' the news and readin' the paper. Nah. It was a suicide all right. You got any evidence says it wasn't?"

"Not enough," she said.

He smiled at her. "Pity. I liked her. Didn't know her well, but admired her. Seemed a good woman, and she sure was a good agency manager. I owe her a lot. In fact, I owe her double, triple maybe. Gettin' out when

she got out is gonna make me richer than the agency ever did in the past, and that wasn't half bad. Gotta admit I had perfect timing this time."

"Getting out when she got out?"

"I didn't mean any disrespect by that. Just a manner of speaking. I really was shocked and sad when I heard she was gone, and gone that way. Depressed me for a while. But I was sure glad I hadn't turned down K.R.C.'s offer. I was about to, but when I heard the news, I sat on it."

Jennifer felt a little sleazy leaving Griffin's office. He had, at first, seemed so bright and optimistic. He fit the image she had built of him from reading the minutes of the meetings.

But in the end he was the same as most of the other financial wizards she knew: out for himself, caring only about the bottom line, the buck. It was disappointing.

She had an evening appointment with Conrad Dennison in his North Sheridan Road office, but a message on her phone answering machine made her call to change that to the next morning.

"Jennifer, this is Jim," the recording said, "and there's an SMS meeting tonight. Check your newspaper's personal column."

With Leo coming back around noon the next day, she wanted to have all her facts straight. It would be bad enough facing him with bad news (and after having opened his mail), but she certainly wanted to have enough information so that she knew for sure whether Samantha Stanton had taken her own life or was murdered.

She didn't need a suspect—just a clue.

Tossing her raincoat over the edge of the couch, she grabbed a piece of chicken from the refrigerator and laid out the newspaper on the table with her other hand.

Jim was right. In among all the love notes and prayers for the now departed, she found a simple message. "SMS tonight. Surf and Turf Inn. Estes Avenue. 7 P.M. Word to the wise."

She didn't want to go alone. She didn't want to be recognized. Of course, she would not use her real name. But Jim couldn't go with her; he was on duty.

Jennifer rummaged around in her closets and trunks for—what was it June Roloff had said?—something frumpy. The clothes and jewelry were easy. Jennifer looked frumpy all right. A bandana in her hair set the tone. But what finished the look was when she found the pink eyeglass frames she had worn in high school, just before she had switched to contact lenses.

She wore her contacts to drive to Estes Avenue off Sheridan, then removed them and put on her old glasses before leaving her car several

blocks from the Surf and Turf. A quick glance in the mirror made her chuckle at the dowdy, middle-aged matron who peeked back.

As Jennifer walked down the rain-swept street, she caught glimpses of herself in the reflections of puddles, but her humor couldn't override her fear.

What if someone recognized her?

What if they asked for identification?

What if she saw someone she knew?

What if they didn't let her out?

What if she forgot what to say when they asked her if she knew what the meeting was about?

But she didn't. "Euthanasia," she said.

"Ten dollars," the woman responded.

"Oh, my," Jennifer said. "I didn't expect that."

"It gets you on our mailing list, honey. And we have expenses. Sign the book up front on the right when you get in the room."

No one seemed to notice when she entered, though forty or so people sat in stacking chairs in a dark-paneled room. She went and stood in line, about sixth, to sign the book. She prayed no one would stand behind her so she'd have time to peek back in the registry to see if she could find Samantha's name—or June Roloff's "Claudia Brown."

But someone came in when Jennifer was second in line. "Go ahead," she said. "I just want to tie my shoe." He passed, and she bent down to tie the old oxford she hadn't worn for years. When she stood, no one was behind her, so she leafed through a few pages before signing, "Louise Purcell."

She didn't see any names she recognized, but she did see a lot of names she assumed were phonies. She had to hand that, at least, to Mrs. Stanton. There was no hiding for her. That's why the escape of suicide seemed so incongruous.

From the looks of the garb and the demeanor, she was guessing she was with a fairly sophisticated intellectual crowd. A spokesman began by passing the notebook around and reminding everybody to add their address so they could be on the mailing list.

As soon she as heard that, Jennifer headed for the back row where she would have time to scan the book without suspicion.

While she waited for the book to make its rounds, a black-bearded man, who appeared to be in his late thirties and who wore an Indian chain and necklace, made an announcement

"For those of you who have been worried about our being found out and hassled and turned away from meeting rooms and such, you'll be happy to know that our lawyers, of whom there are four here tonight—raise your hands; oh, five!—are making real progress with the American Civil

Liberties Union in allowing us to meet in the open and say and do what we want."

There was a certain amount of clapping and subdued cheering. The rest of the surprisingly short meeting consisted of various updates on the chapters in other cities, recent developments in court cases, the sharing of anecdotes about terminally ill patients who suffered unmercifully for years, and more stories of people who were aided in their efforts to die peacefully.

More cheering greeted every such story, and then a list was read of people who belong to the SMS worldwide who had died peacefully, either self-induced or aided, in the last month. There were oohs and aahs when the reader announced that there was a possibility that someone who had attended one of "this very chapter's meetings may have died of her own choosing very recently. It was definitely done to specification and of her own volition."

By then Jennifer was casually looking through the book and unaware of anyone noticing. Sure enough, from the beginning of the book, Samantha Stanton's name appeared on nearly every list. The night they met in Alsip, south on the tollway, a Claudia Brown had signed, but there was no Samantha Stanton.

Jennifer couldn't figure that out and assumed she had missed Samantha's name. She was searching the list one more time when someone nudged her and asked for the book.

On the way home, she detoured farther north on Sheridan Road to check out the address she'd been given for K.R.C. Limited. Her suspicion had been correct. The initials K.R.C. did not appear on the directory in the lobby. The building housed law firms.

Discovering who was represented by Conrad Dennison would be tougher than she thought. She searched the board for his name. It was there alone in suite 4404.

She scanned the board for other names in that same suite. There were three or four listed singly, as Dennison was, and there was another listing of the name of the firm itself, "Cocharan, Thomas, Rand, and Kahill."

*Rand* she thought. *Coincidental? Has to be.* The next morning she asked.

Conrad Dennison got a big belly laugh out of that question. He had come out to the waiting room himself to invite her into his beautifully appointed office, pretty nice for someone who wasn't yet a partner.

"*Yet* is right," he said, sitting at his desk in green suit slacks, white button-down shirt, striped tie, and vest. He also wore alligator cowboy boots. He was in his early forties and had wavy, longish hair that gave

him a slightly outdated look. "If you think this office is nice, you should see the partners' offices."

He made a clicking sound with his mouth to indicate, she supposed, that they were top dog. "But I'll be there soon enough," he said. "Just a matter of time. They take care of me, and I've been doing the job for them for years."

She nodded.

"So you thought Rand was ol' T. J. Rand, did you?" he said, laughing again. "nope, not even close, and am I glad of that! This Rand is one of the Boston Rands," he added, raising his eyebrows as if certain Jennifer would immediately recognize that name. She didn't.

"Tell me about K.R.C.," she said.

He stared evenly at her, not moving. He smiled. "What do you want to know? I thought this had to do with the travel agency."

"Doesn't K.R.C. have anything to do with the travel agency?"

"Well, just in the sense that they own a quarter of it, that's all. I handle that for them."

"Who are they?"

"A holding company. They have several interests."

"Who are they?"

"Business people. A small concern with a lot of irons in a lot of fires. They do well for themselves."

"Who are they?"

"They're private, anonymous people who, if they wanted nosy reporters to know who they were, would have used their names in their logo. Since they didn't, and since I am paid handsomely to represent them in the strictest confidence, you can quit hoping I'll suddenly spew forth the name just because you keep asking."

She stared him down. "Just one name?" she said.

"Name, names what's the difference?"

"The difference is whether it's one person or more than one person. It'll make it easier for me to get the name from public records if I know a little more about this out of-state group."

"You're really being childish for a big city reporter, you know that? You think that by saying they're out-of-state, you're going to get me to think that you really believe that so I'll confirm that they're local. It could be one name and more than one person, you know. Or vice versa."

"Not vice versa," she said sweetly. "That would be stupid. One person and several people's names? Silly."

"Perhaps," he said, reddening. "Do yourself a favor and give up on the name, OK?"

"What do you suppose the odds are that Wilfred Griffin will accept your generous offer?"

Dennison flushed again and clenched his fists. "How do you know about that?"

"I'm a big city reporter," she said.

He softened and smiled, but his fists were still balled. "I'm not at liberty to speak to that either," he said.

"Uncanny sense of timing on that offer," she pressed. "Would you have made it if you'd known?"

"Known what?"

"About Mrs. Stanton."

"I didn't make the offer. I represented it."

"Will you withdraw it now that she's out of the picture?"

"That's none of your business."

# Twelve

Jennifer was desperate, but Dennison didn't know it. And that was all she had to go on. "I've made it my business," she said. "I have to know who's behind K.RC., and if you don't tell me, I'll find out somewhere else."

"What's the big deal?"

"The big deal is that Mrs. Stanton, the majority owner, was murdered, and now here you are making a big play for more of the company for who knows who?"

"Whoa! First, she wasn't murdered! Second, I've always made pitches for more of the company, which a look at any of our records will prove. And third, you'll note that this latest pitch was tendered before she committed suicide. You think it drove her to suicide?"

"Not a chance," Jennifer said. "She was never intimidated by you or the company you represented. And while she was alive, there was no way you could have dreamt of getting more than half the company. Even if you bought out both the other minority partners—which would be foolish because K.R.C. is undoubtedly in collusion with one of them—you would still have only fifty percent."

He sat smiling smugly at her. "Well, if I'm in collusion with another partner, it'd have to be the Rands, wouldn't it?"

She nodded.

"I like the old girl—not so much her ol' man—but she's fun, and we think alike. Unfortunately, she's too shrewd to sell. Maybe if the business flags a little during the transition of managers, the Rands will reconsider."

"There's nothing to the initials relating to the woman's name, is there?" Jennifer tried, feeling foolish.

But Dennison was visibly shaken. "What are you saying?" he managed, eyes narrowing.

"I'm saying I think it's an interesting coincidence that the woman you so enjoy has the initials K. R. Could K.R.C. be the Kirnberly Rand Company?"

"You're joking."

"You're stalling."

"No! Of course not! How could she have me representing her business without her husband's knowledge? Well, let me just say you're not going to get any information out of me, but I'll give you my solemn promise and guarantee, K.R.C. Limited has no more to do with the Rands, either of them, than it does with our own firm."

"And why should I believe you?"

"Maybe you shouldn't. You decide. You're not going to find out one way or the other anyway. But let me save you some time and trouble in your little mission; forget the Rands. I'm serious."

"You only make me want to focus right on them," she said.

He shrugged and raised his hands in surrender. "Suit yourself," he said.

On her way out she paused at the directory board again and stared at the names of the law firm. Cocharan, Thomas, Rand, and Kahill.

Kahill. Rand. Cocharan. Could it be? What would be in it for them without the association with another stockholder? Dennison had said that KR.C. had no more to do with the Rands than it did with his own firm. Maybe there was more truth to that than he intended. But would he have simply handed her that big of a clue?

She needed to talk to someone, and Leo and his son would not be back until about one o'clock. She called Jim, hoping she wasn't waking him. He usually rose by ten or eleven after working the night shift. That would all change when he became a detective. Which would be just before their wedding. *Good timing*, she thought.

"Did I wake you?"

"No, Jenn. I've been up."

"Hungry?"

"Yeah."

"Let's kill two birds with one stone. I need help."

They met at a popular luncheon spot where they found it nearly impossible to talk. They ate quickly and then sat in his car.

"You're right on the button," Jim said. "The problem is, Dennison's offer—on behalf of K.R.C.— made before Samantha's death. But regardless, unless he was aware that the majority stock would fall from fifty to forty upon the execution of Samantha Stanton's will, the purchase doesn't make sense."

"Unless he's just advising K.R.C. that the company will be run better now," Jennifer suggested.

"But he couldn't have known of her death at the time of the offer."

"Or could he?" Jennifer asked.

"Maybe as the representative of K.R.C., Conrad Dennison didn't know," Jim said, warming to her idea. "But K.R.C. knew, whoever they are."

"Can we say that K.R.C. Limited is a suspect—at least one of their people—because they knew of the death in advance and assumed that it would make the sale more attractive?"

"It's a long shot," Jim said, "and the problem is that it points only to greed as a motive."

"What's wrong with that? It's a solid enough motive, isn't it?"

"It's a little galling," he said.

"Granted. But now how do we establish means and opportunity if we don't know who K.R.C. is?"

"We don't. But let's try something."

Jennifer knew not to ask what Jim was up to when he was in that mood with that look on his face. He liked surprises, and he also liked play-by-play announcing them as he went along.

About halfway downtown, he announced that they were going to speak with his soon-to-be superior, Detective Lieutenant Grady Luplo. "He'll know if we have enough to get a warrant to search for the name in private records."

"I implied to Dennison that I would find it in public records," Jennifer said. "But it would also be like looking for a needle in a haystack."

"Were you blufffing, or did you really think you could find it?"

"I don't bluff, you know that."

"Well, you weren't going to find it in public records, and Dennison probably knew that. Don't suppose he gave you much in exchange for that threat."

"Matter of fact, he didn't."

Grady Luplo was an interesting looking character who seemed to enjoy wearing his plainclothes suit, but wearing it less than tidily. The jacket was unbuttoned, and he stood with his hands jammed into the front pockets of his trousers.

"Wow," he said, after a half hour of listening to Jennifer's story and Jim's question. "I don't think so, Jim. No, you haven't nearly enough. There's an awful lot of speculation there, grasping for straws, you know what I mean. I mean, with her buying the drugs herself? I could call my buddy in the D.A.'s office, and he could look up the information for me without a warrant. It wouldn't be totally legal, but—"

"Then we don't want to do it," Jennifer said earnestly.

"Now, wait a minute," Jim said. "I want to get this straight. Is it actually a crime for us just to know this information?"

"No," Luplo said. "It's a crime to use it."

"Is it illegal for you or your friend to dig it out?"

"No. But it can't be used without cause. It'll be thrown out of court. You'll lose your case."

"But the problem is, Lieutenant, that we could use the information to expose a murderer."

"Yeah, you probably could. But if it ever came out that you got the information illegally, you've shot your case on a technicality."

"What would make it legal?"

"The D.A. You want me to call him? I'll call him."

Luplo spoke for several minutes with a contact in the District Attorney's office whom he called Larry. Larry dug out the information for him by computer and read the name to Luplo over the phone. "Thanks, Larry," he said. "I'll probably have to talk to a judge before I can do anything with this, but I'll let you know."

He hung up and turned back to the young couple. "They gave me the name," he said. "I know what it stands for, but I really shouldn't tell you if you're going to pursue this."

"What if we used the name to flush out the killer and got him to admit it himself?" Jim asked.

"Good question. But if it ever came out that you got the information without due cause or a warrant, the case would be jeopardized."

"Did you say name, singular?" Jennifer asked.

Luplo smiled. "I did say that, didn't I?"

"Can you tell me if it's a man or a woman's name?"

"I can tell you that I don't recognize the name. You might, but I don't. It's not a usual name, and I have this feeling that I might have seen or heard it somewhere before, but it doesn't send off any rockets with me."

"Ooh, this is frustrating!" Jennifer said. "That name could be the name of the murderer, someone who had enough knowledge of the business and of Samantha Stanton's life that he or she could have pulled this off. But for what purpose? For what gain?"

"The D.A.'s office agrees we don't have enough, ma'am," Lieutenant Luplo said. "I can ask a judge directly, but they don't like going through us. They prefer their own kind."

"Isn't there a judge in Chicago who was a cop once?" Jim asked.

"Yeah! There is. I'll try him if you want, but you know Saturday is a court holiday. He won't like being bothered at home."

"How long will it take?" Jennifer asked.

"I'd prefer waiting until early afternoon," he said.

"We'd better go, Jim. I've got to meet Leo."

"Yeah. And lover boy Markie."

"Oh, please."

Leo was almost chipper compared to how he had been before he'd gone to Wisconsin. He still had his teary moments, but mostly he was characterized by an attitude that signaled he was ready to get back into the fight.

Jennifer pulled him off to the side to apologize for opening his mail. "Ah!" he said. "It's all right. I was surprised, yeah, and the lawyer was ready to have you fired."

"Really?"

"Yeah! But you know what? I told him to cool his jets. I told him I'd have done the same thing myself. We nosy journalists are all the same. Proves your qualifications."

"It was still wrong, and I'm sorry," she said.

"Granted," he said. "In truth, you owed me that apology, and I accept it." He gave her a little hug. "And I owe you an apology too, or I should say Mark does. You won't get one from him, so it'll have to come from me."

"What are you talking about, Leo?"

"About the way he talked to you on the phone the other night. If he'd been younger, I'd have tanned his hide. He was humiliated to know I overheard him, but I gave him what for anyway. You won't have any more trouble from him."

"Oh, it was all right, Leo. I'm flattered that he was—"

"Nonsense. He knew all along that you were both a widow and engaged. It was foolish and inappropriate, and I told him that. And I apologize."

"I admit I got a little tired of it," she said. "Apology accepted."

By the time she and Jim had filled Leo in on the progress of her investigation, Mark had called a cab and was waiting for his ride to the airport. He was sullen and hadn't looked Jennifer in the eye.

When the cab arrived, Leo stood and embraced his son, both crying. It was difficult for Leo to let go, but the cabbie was honking.

As Mark left, Jennifer thought she saw a look of apology on his face when he finally looked at her. So she smiled her forgiveness, hoping she was guessing right and praying he wouldn't misinterpret the smile.

"Timing," Leo said, as he settled back into his chair. "That's the key to all this stuff. I want to know what you found and when you found it. I'm tellin' you, Jennifer, you're going to get your break when you put it together in sequence and relate it to other events. You'd be surprised how the whys and the whens of what people do are related."

Jennifer looked at lim, wondering if Leo knew what he was saying. "Well, boss," she said, "when I'm finished telling you what all I've found, you may lose the equilibrium you gained with your rest."

"Not good, huh?"

"Not all good, no. Some very confusing and troubling."

He looked woefully at her. "Some of it point to, ah, suicide?"

She nodded. He shook his head slowly. "If it makes any difference to you, Leo, Jim and I are still convinced it was murder."

"Against heavy odds?" he asked.

He held his head in his hands as he heard what she had found at the drugstores. He covered his mouth with his hand when he heard of the diabetes and the glaucoma. He wept when he heard of the meetings she attended.

"It just doesn't sound like her," he said. "Maybe hiding the illness from me. She was always considerate. But this other stuff. It's almost as if someone put her up to it. But nobody could ever put Sam up to anything she didn't want to do."

He sat rocking back and forth, hands on his head. "What in the world have you found to overcome all this evidence?"

She told him of her investigation into the travel agency business. He didn't brighten, but he seemed to listen intently. He agreed there might be something to the name, "and my curiosity is killing me," he said. "When are they going to get back to you on that?"

"Anytime," Jim said. "We hope soon, but if they don't think she's turned up enough evidence, they won't give it to us at all."

"Are you kidding?" Leo said, "Those cops are just like we are. They like a good fight. If they think there's anything in that name, they'll let it out. Either that or they'll go after it themselves."

Realizing a cop was in the room, he winked at Jim. And the phone rang.

# Thirteen

It was Lieutenant Grady Luplo, calling for Jim. He wanted Jim and Jennifer to come back downtown to talk to the judge.

Leo wanted to be in on everything. "I'm tired of hibernating," he said. "Gotta get back in the game. Besides, I can sense you're onto something. This may not be fun, but I want to see it happen—whatever it is."

On the way downtown, Leo wanted to know how Jennifer figured the murderer planted the booklets. "I was afraid you'd ask," she said. "That's the biggest stumper right now, along with the drugstore purchases. It's apparent the pill was made up several days before Samantha died, based on when the ingredients were purchased."

"But how do you explain her buying the ingredients, unless she was despondent over Dr. Billings's diagnosis?"

"I'm not sure of that either," Jennifer said. "Maybe she was forced to buy them, or maybe it wasn't really her. You see, Leo? There's a lot to overcome. I hope the judge doesn't ask the same questions."

"You can bet he will, unless he's in a bad mood. Did they say which judge it was?"

"Ottomeyer," Jim said.

"Crazy old coot," Leo said. "Funny, engaging guy, but coasting. He won't ask a thing, but he'll listen a lot. Be careful not to tell him more than you want to."

Suddenly, Leo was tired. He leaned his head against the window of the back door and tried to sleep. "I can't get past the booklets, the drugstores, and the meetings," he said. "I want to believe what you believe, Jenn, but a gut feeling is all I have."

"And timing," Jim said. "You said it yourself, Leo."

Leo nodded.

Jennifer rifled through her notebook, comparing dates and times and places. "Leo!" she shouted, making everyone jump. "Samantha was out of the country when the drug store purchases were made! Why didn't I see that before?"

Stanton shuddered. "I can hardly believe it," he said. "Even though it's staring me in the face. It *was* murder." He shivered again. "What a feeling," he said, staring out the window. "To think someone would do that to my wife." He added quietly, "Timing."

Jennifer kept reading, flipping pages back and forth and making new notes. Leo grew sullen. "I have to know who," he said, "legally or otherwise. If the judge won't give the police a warrant, I'll get your lieutenant friend to tell me anyway."

"Leo—" Jennifer said.

He held up a hand to silence her, as if to tell her not to even waste her breath.

Leo was right about the judge. He was full of jokes and wisecracks, but he did listen to Jennifer's story of the investigation.

"You'd make a good policewoman, anybody ever tell you that?" the old man cackled.

"My fiancé has told me many times."

"This guy here? You a cop?"

"Yes, sir."

"Good. A detective?"

"Soon," Luplo said.

"Hire the woman instead," the judge said, laughing. He slapped his palms onto his knees and rose unsteadily. "All right," he said, "down to business."

He motioned for Luplo to follow him out into the hall, and as they left, Jennifer heard him begin: "Grady, I'm gonna get a warrant delivered to the D.A.'s office. Now you take over the thing from here and—"

When Luplo returned, he grinned slyly. "Jim," he said, "you can come along on official business. Mr. Stanton and Mrs. Grey, if you're up to it, I need you as decoys."

"Decoys?"

"Yes, ma'am. We may need you to role play to flush out the quarry."

They mapped strategy in the car, and it was four in the afternoon when they arrived at the offices of the *Day*, On the way through the lobby, Jennifer tugged at Leo's sleeve. "The drugs were purchased the day after your promotion was announced," she said.

"Timing," he whispered. "I'm nervous."

"Me too," she said.

When they entered Leo's spacious office next to a conference room on the sixth floor, Luplo was introduced to the secretary, who explained how the intercom worked.

"Let's try it," he said. "Leo, you and Jennifer go into your office and talk in normal tones." After a few seconds, "Ah, that's good. Now, is there a way we can signal that office from out here?"

The secretary showed him a button that emitted a beep so innocuous that the occupants of the office would have to listen for it and know it was coming. "Perfect," he said. "Make the call, Jennifer."

"Mr. Roloff? Jennifer Grey. Fine, thank you, and you? Good. Listen, I'm doing a piece on Mrs. Stanton for the Sunday paper, and I was wondering if you knew whether your wife would be available for a few follow-up questions."

"Follow-up questions?"

"You knew I interviewed her the other day?"

"Ah, no. No, I didn't. But, uh, she's coming to pick me up. We're going out tonight. She should be here any minute. When would you need to talk to her?"

"Right away, if possible, sir."

"Well, we are going out."

"So early? If I could just have, say thirty minutes, I could wrap this up and not have to come in tomorrow. Could you have her call me when she arrives? I'd appreciate it."

There was a pause. "I suppose. You won't be long?"

"Not at all. In fact, Mr. Stanton's secretary has given me permission to use his office, so we'll have complete privacy."

"Oh."

"So she can reach me here. I just want the best friend angle, you understand."

"Sure. I heard Leo had gone to Wisconsin. How's he doing?"

"Under the circumstances, I'd say as well as could be expected."

"Uh-huh. Well, good. Good man. Need him back here. Hey, here's June now!"

"Thanks, Mr. Roloff. I'll be waiting in Mr. Stanton's office."

Leo and Jim and Grady Luplo stepped into a conference room and waited for the secretary's signal that Mrs. Roloff was in with Jennifer. Then they stepped back into the outer office and had the secretary phone Kent Roloff again.

"Mr. Roloff, Mr. Stanton would like to see you in his office, please."

"Leo's back?"

"Yes, sir."

"I didn't know. I mean, when did he get back? Is he all right?"

"He returned this afternoon, and he seems to be doing fine. May I tell him you'll be right up, sir?"

"Absolutely. Is my wife up there?"

"Yes, sir."

Roloff arrived buttoning his coat and straightening his tie. "Leo, man, how are ya?" he said, shaking Leo's hand. "I mean, Mr. Stanton right? Gotta give the boss his due, don't I?"

Leo nodded and smiled weakly. "Kent, this is Lieutenant Grady Luplo, Chicago PD. And you know Jim."

"Nice to meet you—yeah, hi, Jim." Jim nodded. Roloff was still trying to put it all together. "You guys ride home from work together or something?"

"They're here on business, Kent," Leo said. "Let's have a seat right here, huh?"

"What's it all about, Leo? And where's June?"

Leo nodded to his secretary who pressed the button, privately signaling Jennifer that everyone was in place and simultaneously opening the intercom so the four men in the outer office could hear the conversation.

"So I'll start teaching the class on Tuesday nights, and I'm still debating whether to accept an offer to take over the travel agency."

"Who made that offer?" Jennifer asked.

"Well, someone from their board, I guess. I suppose Leo would know him. I'd do it if he thought I should, I guess, but it's hard, you know, like I told you, with all the memories and everything."

"Would you wear a red wig if you ran the agency?" Jennifer asked.

"Pardon me?"

"Would you try to look like Samantha? I mean, it sounds like you're trying to keep her alive by living her life for her."

"I'm not sure what you're driving at," June said, suddenly emotional, "but it's not easy losing your best friend."

"I don't imagine it's easy losing your wife to murder either." Jennifer said.

"You still think it's murder?"

"We know."

"We?"

"We. A serious mistake was made when the murderer bought the ingredients for the fatal dosage, posing as Mrs. Stanton, when Mrs. Stanton was out of the country."

"Really?"

"Really. There was interesting timing there, Mrs. Roloff. It was right around the time of her husband's promotion. Remember when Leo was promoted?"

She nodded.

"Promoted right past your husband?"

"We didn't view it that way. Kent has been at this same level for many years and enjoys it. He's been passed over before. I mean, not passed over. We don't see it as being passed over."

"Anyway, he has enough outside business interests, does he not?"

"Outside? Oh, I suppose. I don't get too much involved in that."

"You don't? The Kent Roloff Company Limited owns a quarter of the stock of the Gateway Travel Agency. And if everything goes as planned, K.R.C. will purchase another twelve and a half percent from Mr. Griffin. When Mrs. Stanton's will is executed, you stand to pick up another ten percent, giving you majority control."

Silence. In the outer office Kent Roloff leaped to his feet and had to be restrained from bursting through the door. He started to yell, but Jim Purcell wrapped his hand around Kent's mouth.

"One thing I can't figure, Mrs. Roloff," Jennifer said. "How you planted the booklets with such excellent timing. I've already figured out that it was you who went to all those SMS meetings, signing Samantha's name each time. And the one time you badgered her into going, she signed the phony Claudia Brown name, and you must have signed something else. I mean, you couldn't get away with signing her name right in front of her, could you?"

Mrs. Roloff licked her lips, but her eyes never wavered. "You figured that out all by yourself, did you?"

Jennifer nodded.

"You get a gold star. You'll never prove anything."

"When handwriting analysis is done, you'll be finished," Jennifer said. "And when the young boy in the drugstore gets a look at you with a red wig. No, you were just a little too eager to have it all at once, you know that?

"You were so jealous, so envious of Samantha that even your friendship couldn't stop you. She always had the spotlight, because she was real. She never had your money, but she had grace you could never muster.

"She saw herself and everyone else as common people. She taught the class. She led the tours. She managed the agency. You were second fiddle. She had the talented and respected husband.

"And when he was promoted over your husband, that was the last straw. You took your knowledge of her illness and put it together with your knowledge of her habits, her shopping, her druggists, her doctor, and even her purse.

"When did you take the opportunity to plant the pill in the bottle, June? Was it when she had to leave the room for a minute and was trusting you to watch it, the way we do with the one person we know we can trust?

"Did you wait on pins and needles, and for how long, before she finally got enough headaches and got around to the fatal pill? Did you ever wonder if you should grab the bottle and change your mind?"

Mrs. Roloff shook her head. She had worked up tears the first time around. None were necessaly now.

"C'mon," Jennifer said. "Tell me about the booklets. How did you plant them at just the right time?"

June Roloff sighed heavily. "That was just luck," she said softly. "I gave them to her about a week before and asked her to hold them for me because I knew Kent wouldn't want them in the house. He wouldn't even want to know I had them. She said Leo wouldn't either, but I said Kent had even been known to go through my purse. She said Leo had never once gotten near her purse, even when she asked him to bring her something from it. So she kept them for me in her purse. Twice she told me she was bringing them back, and I asked her to just wait another week."

"She waited long enough, didn't she?" Jennifer said.

Mrs. Roloff nodded. "Kent had nothing to do with this, you know."

Jennifer flinched. "Are you serious?"

"Yes. He didn't know I was getting ten percent of the company. He knew I owned a quarter through the private corporation, and we kept that from the Stantons over the years. But everything else was on my own. He knew nothing of it."

Jennifer shook her head in disbelief.

"Oh, it's true," Mrs. Roloff said in a monotone, staring straight ahead. "And you almost assessed it correctly too."

"Almost?"

"Almost."

"Where was I off?"

"The reasons."

"Not jealousy?"

"Oh, I suppose. But it was Leo I wanted, not Samantha's life. Not her beauty. Not her visibility. Not her job or her teaching or her travels. I wanted him."

"Did he ever know that?"

"Never. I never had the nerve to make a pass at him. Too much character there. In him, not me."

"How was this going to get Leo for you?"

"Oh, I was only halfway there when you stepped in."

"You mean—?"

"Uh-huh. Only half the job was done."

"Your husband—?"

She nodded. "—would have been next."

When Jennifer reached the outer office, she fell into Jim's arms. June Roloff walked past two weeping men, both slumped in chairs. And into the custody of Lieutenant Grady Luplo, Chicago PD.

Flip over for another great mystery!
TOO LATE TO TELL